George Combe

The Currency Question

Anatiposi

George Combe

The Currency Question

Reprint of the original, first published in 1858.

1st Edition 2023 | ISBN: 978-3-38231-518-4

Anatiposi Verlag is an imprint of Outlook Verlagsgesellschaft mbH.

Verlag (Publisher): Outlook Verlag GmbH, Zeilweg 44, 60439 Frankfurt, Deutschland
Vertretungsberechtigt (Authorized to represent): E. Roepke, Zeilweg 44, 60439 Frankfurt, Deutschland
Druck (Print): Books on Demand GmbH, In de Tarpen 42, 22848 Norderstedt, Deutschland

THE

CURRENCY QUESTION,

CONSIDERED IN RELATION TO

THE ACT OF THE 7TH & 8TH VICTORIA, CHAP. 32.

COMMONLY CALLED

THE BANK RESTRICTION ACT.

By GEORGE COMBE.

AUTHOR OF "THE CONSTITUTION OF MAN," ETC., ETC.

———◆———

TENTH EDITION.

REVISED BY THE AUTHOR, WITH
COMMENTS UPON THE PRESENT SUSPENSION OF
THE BANK-CHARTER ACT,
AND
REMARKS UPON THE BANK NOTE QUESTION
IN SCOTLAND.

———◆———

LONDON:
EFFINGHAM WILSON, ROYAL EXCHANGE.
EDINBURGH:—ADAM & CHARLES BLACK, NORTH BRIDGE.
—
1858.

PREFACE.

THE following pages on the " Currency Question" and " the Bank Restriction Act" of 1844, were written for the *Scotsman* newspaper, by desire of the Editor, and appeared in its columns in November and December, 1855, and February, 1856. They attracted so much attention that a separate impression of them, in the pamphlet form, was taken from the newspaper types, and was speedily sold. A new impression has been demanded, and is now presented to the public.

From 1810 to 1837, I was placed in circumstances that enabled me practically to observe the influences of Banking and of Bank-note circulation on the fortunes of manufacturers and merchants; and I was often employed in business negociations between bankers and these two classes of practical men. I passed part of the year 1838, the whole of 1839, and part of 1840, in the United States of North America, when a most disastrous monetary crisis took place. Being conversant with the principles and practice of Scotch Banking, I had frequent opportunities of discussing the American system with leading bankers and merchants of New York, Boston, and Philadelphia; and watched closely the phenomena of the currency of the States during these years. The views now published, therefore, were drawn, not so much from abstract principles, as from practical observations; while, at the same time, I did not neglect the study of the writings of political economists on the subject. I was particularly impressed by the luminous expositions of it given forth from time to time by Mr. Jones Loyd, now Lord Overstone, who treated it with the skill of a master, combining practical knowledge with scientific principle, in a manner rarely exhibited in the controversies to which it has given rise.

GEO. COMBE.

45, Melville-street, Edinburgh,

CONTENTS.

From "THE TIMES" (City Article) of March 4, 1856.

"A SERVICE has been rendered to the commercial public, and to all persons desirous of obtaining a concise exposition of the principles and operation of the Bank Charter Act of Sir Robert Peel, by the republication, as a pamphlet, of the series of articles on 'The Currency Question,' recently contributed to the *Scotsman* nswspaper by Mr. George Combe. Its great merit is, that it supplies the want, constantly felt by many intelligent persons, of a concise and logical statement, to save them from wading though the mass of contradictory treatises daily poured forth upon the subject, and commonly supposed by modest inquirers to be profound in proportion as they are incomprehensible. No such work has hitherto been attainable. Lord Overstone, to whom Sir R. Peel was indebted for the philosophy upon which he acted, has expounded from time to time the entire principles of the system; but his writings, together with those of Mr. Norman, Colonel Torrens, and Sir Charles Wood, have appeared at intervals, as the necessity of the occasion demanded, and not in a collective form so as to be available for the uninstructed reader, desirous for the first time of grasping the argument as a whole. Mr. Combe's pamphlet fulfils, in this respect, everything that could be required; and, to their surprise, it will show many who have been deterred from the topic by regarding it as something only to be mastered by the experience of a life, that it involves nothing but what may in half an hour be comprehended by any mind free from the incurable hallucination, that there is some method for Governments to create at pleasure 'a sufficient supply of the circulating medium.' It will at the same time, until its broad and simple doctrines shall have been controverted, leave no excuse for those who may continue to trouble the community with incessant effusions on the matter, indicating nothing except a unanimity of disagreement, and that the maze in which each struggling theorist is lost, is an independent one of his own creation."

—————

From "THE MORNING POST" (City Article of March 31, 1856).

"We have another edition of Mr. George Combe's treatise on the great money question now before us. Mr. Combe's pamphlet on the currency may be termed the alphabet of monetary science. It has, we understand, passed through six editions in less than a month—a circumstance not of frequent occurrence in the history of currency writings. When it is considered that the fluctuations in the circulating medium of any country affect materially the prices of every article of consumption, the paramount importance of knowing the moving cause becomes prominently apparent. Every merchant, trader, and banker, and every banker's clerk, can now master this subject without much trouble, as it is here rendered perfectly easy; and without much cost of time, as in this single pamphlet the whole question can be examined in less than an hour."

THE CURRENCY QUESTION.

[*From the Scotsman of November* 21, 1855.]

THE Edinburgh Chamber of Commerce has petitioned Lord Palmerston "to advise the immediate suspension of the Act 7 and 8 Victoria, chap. 32," commonly called the Bank Restriction Act, "with a view to its ultimate repeal." The grounds of this request are, that the Act is at present "exercising an injurious influence on the trade and commerce of the country; that though this Act was intended to secure the country against a panic in monetary affairs, it has proved, both in 1847 and at the present moment, to have an exactly opposite effect; and, in the opinion of your memorialists, nothing short of the interposition of the executive can prevent the most disastrous consequences arising from its continued operation."

On previous occasions we have largely entered into this question; but as it seems difficult to maintain its real merits steadily before the public mind, and as it is one of vital importance, we feel constrained to enter again into the consideration of it; and we shall endeavour to do so in the language and spirit of common sense, avoiding as much as possible technical terms and abstract arguments.

The "currency" simply means a thing which all persons shall consent to use as a medium of exchange in buying and selling. It is also called "a standard of value," because the "price" of every commodity bought and sold is measured by it. Prices are said to "rise," when we must give an increased amount of currency for the things bought; and to "fall," when we obtain them for a smaller amount.

In the present instance, for the sake of elucidation, we may divide buyers and sellers into two classes: *First*, Those who reside in our own kingdom, and are governed by the same laws; and, *Secondly*, Foreign nations who have no connection with Great Britain, except as voluntary buyers and sellers in her markets.

The members of the British community, in buying and selling among themselves, may use anything as a standard of value or currency in which *they all* have confidence — no matter whether it be paper, gold, or cowries. But if they select a thing for currency that may be increased or diminished in quantity arbitrarily, the prices of commodities bought and sold by it will rise when it is increased, and fall when it is diminished in quantity, as arbitrarily as its quantities are varied. The problem, therefore, is to find a thing which cannot be arbitrarily increased and diminished in quantity, and one also in which *all* shall have perfect confidence ; for if the quantities vary arbitrarily, prices vary arbitrarily ; and if confidence is not universal, its utility as currency ends where the confidence fails. If Yorkshire, for example, should decline to sell its goods to be paid for in the thing which Edinburgh employs as its currency, or *vice versâ*, commerce between those places could not be carried on, and barter would be the only resort. If, therefore, we select paper as our sole internal medium of exchange, it must be paper which shall not arbitrarily vary in quantity, and which also shall be received as of the same value from Caithness to Devonshire, and from Londonderry to Limerick and Cork. Is this what the Chamber of Commerce desires Lord Palmerston to supply ? If it be so, why do they not tell him *how* to find it ? Let us hear what they recommend.

They inform his Lordship, that they " do not object to the principle of stipulating, on the part of the public, *for security* from those intrusted *with supplying the paper* currency of the realm ; but they do most emphatically object to the plan of restricting that security to the possession of gold alone." Let us ask them, then, whether they desire the *quantity* of the paper currency to be increased *ad libitum* by those intrusted with supplying it, on the sole condition that they shall give to the public securities equal to its amount ? And, secondly, as they emphatically object to restricting the security to the possession of gold, what other things they propose to be taken as securities ?

To render the answers intelligible, let it be borne in mind that the bank note is a promise to pay one, five, twenty, or a hundred *pounds* to the holder on demand. If the security is gold sovereigns, the promise *can* be redeemed if the bank possesses gold in proportion to its issues; but the memorialists object to this, and desire some other article of value to be pledged as security.

What, then, shall it be ? Shall it be acres of land, houses, mills and machinery, colonial produce, pig-iron, railway stocks, government stocks, or merchants' bills and promissory notes ? We suspect that the latter are what the Chamber has chiefly in view, and that they desire paper-currency to be increased in proportion to the mercantile bills presented for discount ; but let us assume that the former things may be taken as securities, do they mean that the paper-currency shall be increased to any extent as long as these things, or any of them, are offered and taken as securities ? If they do so, and as they object to the issuers of the notes being *bound to pay in gold*, the form of the note must be varied into " I promise to pay *in securities* equivalent in value to five pounds." We ask, " Equivalent to five pounds of value in what ?" As the Chamber excludes gold, shall the payment be made in tea, in broadcloth, in acres, in machinery, or in what ? This question *must be answered*, because if the notes are not to be payable in gold, they must be payable in something else, otherwise they would be mere waste paper, and nobody would buy and sell by them. But if they be made payable in a thing that *everybody* cannot use again as currency, they are not serviceable for purposes of commerce. They will not be received by those who cannot pay their own debts with them. Now, we ask, would notes payable in acres of land in Scotland, be received as currency in England or Ireland, or *vice versâ* ?

In the next place, will the Chamber of Commerce point out how the arbitrary increase of the paper-currency can be prevented, if the only restriction on the issue of it is to consist in the deposit of securities ? On this principle we may have a paper-currency equal in quantity to the estimated value of the whole property of the country ; and if so, what would be the value of such a currency ?

These may appear to be abstract arguments ; but, in point of fact, the very thing which the Chamber of Commerce recommends has been practically tried in the United States of North America—and we shall describe the results of the experiment.

Some of the States passed Acts by which a public comptroller was authorised to take from any individuals or associations of persons wishing to issue bank notes, pledges of State Stocks, yielding dividends, and " mortgages upon improved, productive, and unencumbered lands," and to give them in return notes certified by him as thus secured, to be used by them at their own discretion as currency.

The articles pledged, although hypothecated to the comptroller, remained the property of the currency vendors, who drew the profits and dividends of them for their own advantage, as long as no demand was made on the comptroller for liquidation of the notes. The annual returns of the things pledged may be stated at 7 per cent. ; and the bank notes, when lent out in discounting bills, or on mortgages, brought other 7 per cent.—this being the common rate of interest in the United States.

Jonathan was not slow in discerning that this was a capital speculation. For 100,000 dollars of capital, he obtained the profits of 200,000 dollars, *minus* the expenses of the paper on which his notes were printed, and those of his establishment of cashiers, clerks, and porters, for carrying on the circulation.

There was immediately a rush towards pledging " securities" and issuing bank notes, and money became exceedingly abundant ; the price of every commodity rose with a rapidity corresponding to the issue of the notes ; every man who bought and sold, believed himself enriched. In New York, the bottom of the sea next to the streets was actually mapped into lots, and became a subject of extensive dealing.

In our country, similar results would inevitably ensue from similar proceedings. If the things hypothecated for security for the currency yielded a revenue, and if the currency-makers were allowed to draw *it*, and at the same time the profits of its value in currency-notes, a direct inducement would be given to them to swell their issues as extensively as possible; and from obtaining a double return for their capital, they could afford to encounter risks in doing so, which no capitalist enjoying only a single return could face. They would naturally, therefore, become the patrons of adventurers and speculators, who would circulate their notes extensively, and keep them long afloat. Such issues would certainly have the effect of raising the price of commodities to an extent corresponding to their amount.

The Chamber of Commerce will, we hope, acknowledge that, according to their views, America was then a commercial paradise. Bank notes issued *ad libitum*, security not questioned, and confidence universal! What more could be desired? But America consists of different States, as Britain does of different kingdoms; and, like Britain, it also trades with foreign nations. The people of Ohio and Missouri, whose pockets were full of paper-currency, gave very large orders for goods to the merchants of New York, Boston, and Philadelphia, who duly executed them. The bills given for the purchases were payable in those eastern cities; and when the western debtors went to their own bankers for bills of exchange on those places in return for their own local currency, the bankers discovered that their home customers had bought more from the eastern cities than they had sold; that they had already drawn on the east for every dollar which the east was indebted to them, and could draw no more. The western merchants then sent their own currency notes to the eastern cities in payment; but unfortunately for them, the merchants there had already paid all they owed to the west, and nobody in New York or Philadelphia wanted western notes for any purposes of use, and nobody was disposed to travel six or seven hundred miles to request the cashiers of the western States to pay their notes, or, in those States in which security had been given, to require the comptroller to sell the pledged securities and pay them the *money* produce. Moreover, every one knew that it was physically impossible in either case to obtain the amounts in money; for *there was no currency* in which the pledged property, when sold, could have been paid, *except bank notes*, resting on securities or on the mere promise of the banker.

Jonathan now found himself *in a fix*, and became alarmed. A friend was in Albany at the time, and intended to visit Cincinnati. He obtained as many Cincinnati bank notes as he desired, at a discount of twenty-five per cent., in exchange for New York bank notes, which were still paid in gold. These western notes were then current in Ohio as sound currency, and he used them as such in paying his travelling expenses. What followed? When the eastern merchants declined to receive the western notes in payment, the very evil which the Chamber of Commerce asserts to be the result of the obligation on the Bank of England to redeem its notes in gold actually ensued. Every one rushed to the banking-houses and demanded *payment* of the notes in specie; for the notes bore to be payable, not in securities, but in dollars. The bankers had neither gold nor silver; and those who had pledged stocks and given mortgages for their issues, told the holders that the Comptrollers held securities, and that the notes were perfectly safe, and equal in value to dollars in hard cash. Jonathan, however, could not believe this, for two reasons, which bear directly on our present circumstances, and which we shall state in the course of some further remarks we intend to offer on the subject.

[*From the Scotsman of November* 24, 1855.]

In speaking on Wednesday of the present aspect of the Currency question, in relation to the recent strange resolutions of the Edinburgh Chamber of Commerce, we used as illustration the experience of the United States, and brought up the narrative to the point at which Jonathan found that the banks could give him neither silver nor gold for the notes, but referred him to the amount of " securities," such as state stock and mortgages, which they had deposited in the hands of the " Public Comptroller." Let us now see the two reasons—reasons bearing closely on our own circumstances at this moment—for which Jonathan found himself unable to believe these assurances : —

1st. He found that bank notes secured on property situated in one state did not command confidence in another. In like manner, bank notes not payable in specie, but secured on Scotch property, would not command confidence in England and Ireland, and *vice versâ*. 2ndly. Jonathan had bought to a larger amount than he had sold in the markets of Europe, and he discovered that nobody in Europe would receive his bank notes, secured or unsecured, in payment of the balances due by him. In a similar way, bank notes not payable in gold, but secured *on property situated in Great Britain*, would not be received as currency in France, Germany, the United States, Italy, India, and China — (the notes of the Bank of England are now received by the money-changers and the bankers of the Continent only because they *are* payable in gold). When, therefore, Britain owed a balance to these nations, or wished to buy from them at a time when they did not desire to buy from her, if she had nothing to offer them except bank notes not payable in gold, but only secured on British property, her commerce with them would come altogether to a close.

We have not yet, however, exhausted the American experiment. The enormous rises in the prices of goods and property of every description, consequent on the issue of bank notes, led the merchants of the commercial ports of the United States to give very large orders for goods in Europe. At the same time, these extravagant prices deterred the European merchants from buying largely in the American markets. The consequence was the creation of a large balance due by America to Europe. The American bank notes were of no avail in paying this balance; but for a time Jonathan sent the bonds of his States in payment, and as these were taken freely by capitalists in Europe for investments, they, for some time, served as a means of paying American debts to European merchants. The bonds, however, came in such overwhelming quantities, that European capitalists became alarmed about their value, and ceased to purchase them. The American merchants then besieged their bankers for gold in payment of their notes, with a view to send it to Europe in extinction of their debts. The banks of Massachusetts, Connecticut, and New York, had contracted their issues in time, and accumulated specie, and paid their notes in gold to the last. Most of the banks in the other States had relied on "confidence" and "securities," and had not taken these precautions, and consequently had no gold to give for their notes. They passed a *de facto* "Bank Restriction Act," for they suspended cash payments without professing insolvency. And what followed? According to our Chamber of Commerce, this practical Bank Restriction Act should "have secured the country against a panic in monetary affairs;" but it had a diametrically opposite effect. The demand for gold had arisen from the necessity of paying debt to countries which declined to receive bank notes; and while the bank notes of the three States just mentioned, which could be exchanged for gold, continued to be received as equal in value to gold, the bank notes of Pennsylvania and other States, whose banks had suspended specie payments, fell to a large discount. In 1839, the bank notes of Philadelphia, current in that city, were at a discount of thirteen per cent. in New York; and every man who owed 100 dollars in New York was under the necessity of giving his banker 113 dollars of Philadelphia currency for a bill of exchange to that amount. The bank notes of Misssouri were at a discount of thirty per cent. compared with those of New York, and the rate of exchange was 130 dollars in Missouri currency for every 100 dollars payable in that city.

Another consequence ensued. When the bank notes ceased to be redeemed in gold, every one lost confidence in them; and when those who had issued them on "securities" offered those securities for sale, nobody in the suspending States had a currency of the value of gold in which to pay for them, and nobody was *willing* to sell for depreciated bank paper. The prices of all stocks and property, measured by gold, or by the paper of gold-paying banks, fell as rapidly as they had previously risen. Ruin enveloped every man who was in debt, for his creditors *forced* him to sell as long as he possessed any saleable commodity; and the pressure of sales and paucity of purchasers brought prices to the lowest ebb. So far did the ruin extend, that almost all the banks of Pennsylvania, including the United States' Bank, with a capital of seven millions sterling paid up, failed; and actually there was not a currency in that state which commanded "confidence" adequate to the daily wants of the community in trade. In the country, the people were forced to resort to barter; and in the city of Philadelphia, the solvent merchants gave orders on the few banks that remained solvent, which the bank on which it was drawn marked as " good ;" and the others took it as money, crediting the person who presented it in their books, and debiting the bank on which it was drawn with the amount. The banks settled between themselves the balances arising on these transfers as they were best able."*

The fall of prices, and consequent ruin, were not confined to the bank-suspending States. The bankers of New York, Connecticut, and Massachusetts, who continued to pay gold for their notes, did so only by diminishing the quantity of them in circulation ; in other words, by declining to accommodate with loans or discounts customers who were unable to pay for the large stocks of goods which they held. These customers were, consequently, forced to dispose of their stocks at very depreciated prices, frequently involving them in insolvency, and thus the evil was equally wide-spreading and disastrous.

How did this convulsion terminate ? The insolvent merchants, and their impoverished customers in the west, limited their purchases in the east to the barest necessaries, and laboured hard until they had sent produce to the Atlantic cities to an amount whch rendered these cities debtors to them. They then resumed their purchases to the extent of the balance in their favour. The Atlantic cities, again, limited their purchases from Europe to a low amount, and sent forward as much produce as they could command for sale in the European markets, until the balance was again turned in their favour, and then gold was returned to them in liquidation of it. The return of gold enabled the banks to extend their issues, prices of commodities rose in proportion to the amount of gold returned, and the increase of bank circulation and prosperity again dawned on the Union.

Shall this example, and all the demonstrated conclusions of the profoundest thinkers, and most experienced practical men in Parliament and out of it, tested during half a century, be abandoned on the mere assertions of the men who, in this instance, have led the Chamber of Commerce ? We know that there is no panic at present among our people, inducing them to draw and hoard gold. The demand for it, therefore, is for exportation. Now, this demand cannot arise unless England is in debt to the countries to which the gold is sent; and it is easy to discover how this has happened. We are buying food and raw produce abroad extensively, and the Government is spending largely in foreign conntries : and while this is going on, prices are so high at home that foreign purchases in our markets have declined ; and our exports, in relation to our imports and to the Government expenditure, taken together, have diminished. The contraction of the currency will force us to limit our purchases abroad, and it will also cause the prices of goods to fall at home ; the consequence of which fall will be increased purchases by foreigners in our markets, and the balance of trade will turn in favour of England, after which gold will again return.

As no mortal power can avert this sequence of causes and effects, the inconsiderateness with which public bodies commit themselves

* See Note on page 39.

to opinions they have not weighed, is most injurious to the welfare of the country, and to their own weight with Parliament and their fellow-citizens. They appear to do this at the instigation of those of their members who, apparently, are the least capable of leading them to sound conclusions. Do they not perceive that gold is recommended as a currency, and also as a security for bank-issues, by the following advantages?—1st. It cannot be increased and diminished in quantity *arbitrarily*; 2ndly. It is accepted as a standard of value, and as a medium of payment by all trading nations, foreign and domestic; and 3rdly. While held as a security for paper-issues it yields no return itself, and thus removes the temptation to increase the issues for the sake of the double profit—first, the revenue of the security; and secondly, the interest on the notes issued.

In this instance, the Edinburgh Chamber has made no attempt to grapple with the principles of the currency question; and, apparently from not comprehending these, they have drawn erroneous inferences from the few facts and figures which they quote. It is absurd to be always assuming that, in a question such as this, the Legislature, which has no separate or sinister interest, after the most anxious inquiry and deliberation, makes and maintains laws designed to impede or injure commerce. The causes, we repeat, which regulate the phenomena of currency and exchange, are as completely natural and as certain in their operations as the force of gravitation itself; and it is folly to ignore these in the way exhibited in this memorial. It is only by omitting the principles, or misinterpreting the facts, that confusion can be created on this subject; and how can we expect effect to be given to the petition of persons who obviously do not know what or wherefore they are asking?

[From the Scotsman of November 28, 1855.]

In two former notices we dealt with the *principles* of the currency question. We shall now advert to the facts on which the Edinburgh Chamber of Commerce found their petition. They inform Lord Palmerston that—

"Your memorialists strenuously opposed the passing of the Act 1844, as an unsafe and an unwise interference with the business of banking, and directly calculated, in the event *of a scarcity of food, war, or any other emergency, requiring an export of gold,* to give rise to commercial embarrassments and arousing panics; and *when in* 1847 *these actually began to appear, they denounced the Act as the cause,* and that Government was at length constrained to suspend its operation—thus substantially acknowledging the correctness of the views of your memorialists."

It would be difficult to condense into the same space a greater collection of fallacies and misstatements than this paragraph contains. The Chamber commence by acknowledging that "a scarcity of food," "war," or "any other emergency," *may* require "an export of gold." This is solid sense; and we ask them, how do these events *come to require an export of gold?* Obviously, because we are in debt to foreign nations for corn; for furnishings to our soldiers and sailors engaged in war in foreign parts; and also for silks, tea, coffee, sugar, cotton, flax, and other articles sold to us by them, and consumed in our families, or used as raw materials in our manufactories. As long as we export to these nations manufactured goods, or other articles of value, to an amount equal to the value of our purchases from them, the transactions balance each other, and are settled by bills of exchange negotiated by bankers. Suppose English merchants were to buy wheat in America to the value of a million of pounds sterling, and to grant bills for the amount payable in London, and that American merchants should buy English hardware to the same extent, and grant bills for it payable in New York—these bills would be carried by the merchants who received them to the bankers of their respective countries: the London bankers would send the American acceptances to the bankers of New York, to be placed to their credit with them; and the New York bankers would send the English acceptances to London, to be placed to their credit in that city. The two sets of bills would furnish funds of credit— one for England in America, and one for America in England, each of equal amount, on which the bankers could draw bills of exchange; and in settling these transactions it would be unnecessary to transmit gold to either country.

In 1846, however, the potato blight brought a famine on Ireland, and greatly raised the price of food all over the United Kingdom. Our merchants, therefore, bought grain in every foreign country where they could obtain it; and it was necessary that they should pay for it. The blight was a sudden and unexpected calamity, and the demand for corn which it occasioned in foreign countries was quite unexpected. The natives of these countries did not change their habits of living as suddenly as this demand arose, but continued for some time to buy only their usual quantities of goods in the English markets. English merchants, therefore, became debtors to foreign merchants to a larger amount than the foreign merchants were debtors to them, and it became necessary to discharge this balance. As shown in our former remarks, the foreign merchants would not accept of bank-notes for this balance, even although secured on Government Stock, or acres of land, or any other thing fixed in Great Britain, because these merchants did not need such securities or commodities for any purpose of their own; they could not buy with them in other markets, nor pay their own debts with them. The Chamber of Commerce, however, objected (and they actually boast of their wisdom in doing so) to the Bank of England being bound to pay gold to the merchants who owed this balance, and who held in their hands bank notes equal to its amount; but the Chamber omitted to tell us what was to be done. The foreigners declined to accept bank-notes, but were willing to accept gold in payment. The Chamber, in their wisdom, said, "No; do not give the merchants gold for these notes, with which to pay their foreign debts." What, then, was to be done? The Chamber acknowledge our liability to get into debt to foreign nations for value received, and they object to the Bank furnishing the merchants who hold bank-notes with the only thing which the foreigners will receive in payment. Do they mean, then, that we should swindle the foreigners, "repudiate" and not pay our debts? Are they incapable of conceiving that these nations may not need our goods at the very moment and to the exact extent to which we require their supplies, and that thus a balance may arise against us? And we again ask the Chamber, How is this balance to be paid, if those who have issued paper-currency are not to be bound to redeem it in gold when it is needed to be sent to other countries where their paper is of no value? It is a stipulated condition, that when the holder of bank-notes finds it impossible to use them in his transactions, the bankers shall liquidate them in the thing which they have engaged to pay, and which he *can* make use of in his trade.

It happened, moreover, that in 1845-6, just before the blight, the nation had become excited by a railway mania. Hundreds of millions were suddenly sunk in the construction of these works; a large expenditure took place in wages; and the working-classes, thus enriched, consumed colonial produce to an unusual extent. The extra importation of this produce ran us in debt to the colonies. Farther, we bought shares in French and other foreign railways to the amount of hundreds of thousands of pounds; and these also required to be paid for abroad. Again, the sudden inflation of railway shares, and the gambling speculations which infected all classes, from the duchess to the dairymaid, produced a temporary belief in these individuals that they had become suddenly rich, and led them into extravagant expenditure in silks, satins, jewellery, wines, fruits, and other expensive articles of foreign produce, so that England ran in debt to the whole world who had anything tempting to taste or avarice to sell.

While this was proceeding, the expenditure, of the working-classes, and of genteel speculators in articles of domestic manufacture also, was enormous. Prices rose high, and, in consequence, we sold fewer of these commodities than usual to foreigners. Trade, however, was brisk; every one imagined himself prosperous; and, as confidence was complete, bank paper was increased in amount in proportion to the extent of the transactions going forward; and this state of things continued for some time. Towards the end of 1847 and the beginning of 1848, however, it became necessary to pay the balances due to foreigners; and the British merchants found themselves in an awkward position for doing so. During the railway mania, prices of all articles had risen so much, that the manufacturers and merchants had increased their stocks to the utmost limit, not of their capital only, but of their credit. The great majority of traders thus held heavy stocks, and were in debt both at home and abroad. The railway speculators also had bought more shares than they had money to pay for, and they, too, were in debt. Here, then, many were in debt and encumbered with goods and shares; and the problem was, how to get out of this awkward position?

The Chamber affirm that it was the obligation to pay gold imposed by the Bank Restriction Act, which was "*the cause*" of this state of things and of its consequences. Never was there a grosser perversion of facts. As long as England was not in debt to foreigners, and as manufacturers, merchants, and railway-makers kept within the limits of their own capital, everything proceeded prosperously and smoothly. There was no panic, no inflation of prices, no rush for gold, and trade was steady and yielded a fair profit. It was the calamity of the blight, and speculative excitement leading to an enormaus expenditure of money—much of it raised on credit—both unfortunately occurring at the same time, that plunged so many people into debt. Had the Bank of England not paid its notes in gold, our merchants, who were indebted to foreigners, but who were still solvent and had balances in the Bank, must have suspended payment of necessity; and as those merchants who were engulphed in debt actually suspended, the run and desolation would have become universal.

The Bank directors had a hard struggle to maintain. These debtors came to them in flocks, with states of their affairs in their hands showing the value of their stocks, now unsaleable, and the amount of their debts, and argued, that if they could only be accommodated with a loan of bank notes until the market revived, they should avoid bankruptcy, and prevent a general crash. By this they meant that the Bank should take their goods in pledge, and give them bank notes in return. But the directors found that, until the balance due to foreigners was extinguished, every note they issued re-appeared in a few days, accompanied by a demand for gold for transmission abroad. They saw their stock of gold diminishing with great rapidity, and they had no means of ascertaining how far the balance due to foreigners was from being liquidated. No alternative, therefore, was left to them, as honest men, but to decline issuing notes on the pledge of unsaleable goods and stocks. They gave warning of this necessity from week to week by raising the rate of discount in proportion to the pressure of the demand for gold; and this high rate, joined to their refusal to issue notes on pledged goods, led to extensive failures among men of all classes — manufacturers, merchants and railway speculators — *who were in debt* beyond the limits of their *tangible capital*.

That portion of the community which was in debt, many of them members of the Chambers of Commerce, Town Councils, and other incorporations, now tried to screen their own errors, and save their own credit, by raising the cry that the obligation on the Bank of England to pay gold for its notes *was the cause* of all these dire events ; and they succeeded in inducing other persons to take up the cry. A panic seized the British people, and there was a run on the banks generally for gold, for domestic hoarding. On the 27th of October, 1847, the Government authorised the Bank to suspend payments to tranquillise them; but they did this solely because the insane terror and misapprehension which prevailed could be met in no other way. The Bank directors, however, understood the circumstances, and what was meant The mere announcement of the permission to suspend, dissipated the terror; the run for gold for domestic hoarding ceased; and the *operation* of the Act of 1844, as a means of supplying gold for paying English debts to foreigners, *never was suspended*. It performed all its beneficial functions with perfect success, and was seen to have done so the moment the public mind was tranquillised by the promise that it should be set aside if necessary. We are assured by one who has the means of knowing that Mr. John Macfarlan's statement in his speech to the Chamber, that "the private bankers of London intimated [he does not say *to whom*] that if the Act was not suspended, they would withdraw their balances," is wholly unfounded.

The evil consequences of the state of things now described were aggravated by another unexpected occurrence. In February, 1848, Louis Philippe was chased from the French throne, and a wild democracy established in his place. Political revolutions followed in quick succession in almost every country of Europe; and in April of that year the Chartists threatened to sack London. Great additional monetary embarrassments arose out of these events. Nevertheless, the domestic panic having been assuaged, the Bank never faltered in meeting the demand for gold for exportation. In point of fact, it disappeared when our impoverished people ceased to over-buy foreign produce, and tempted foreigners, by low prices, to buy from them.

But dark as this picture of ruin and desolation is, it has another side, which we shall exhibit in our next article.

[*From the Scotsman of December* 5, 1855.]

We concluded our last observations on the Currency by the remark, that the dark picture of commercial ruin and desolation of 1847-8 had a brighter side; and we now solicit attention to it. The great sufferers on that occasion were the improvident persons who had bought or manufactured goods, or purchased shares or other property beyond their means of paying for them, and the creditors who had imprudently trusted them. When the directors of the Bank of England paid gold for their notes, they were very cautious in re-issuing them. to prevent their being immediately presented again for more gold. The country bankers, who also were bound to pay in gold, were forced to follow their example, and the consequence was a great diminution of the currency This and the forced sales following on bankruptcies, produced a rapid fall in the prices of all commodities held by the debtor class. Every one, however, who had avoided speculative entanglements, and had prudently husbanded his capital, now entered the markets with great advantage, and bought shares and goods, mills, houses, and machinery, at very low prices. Annuitants, and persons living on the interest of capital, found their condition greatly improved; for money being scarce, interest rose; and as goods had fallen, their incomes became from 20 to 30 per cent. more valuable than in the days of the mania—that is to say, they received a higher rate of interest, and the money they drew served to purchase more goods in the shops. Prudent retail traders also did not suffer; for although they were forced to sell their stocks at lower prices, they were able to replace them at rates correspondingly low, and they had the benefit of a rise when commercial prosperity returned.

The fall of prices, also brought foreign purchasers largely into our markets, and we being no longer able to buy equally from them, they ran into debt to us. What would the Edinburgh Chamber of Commerce have thought, had their brethren in the Chambers of Commerce of New York and Paris, who had bought goods in England which they could not readily sell at home, and could not easily pay for, petitioned their legislatures to prevent their bankers from paying gold to be remitted to England in extinction of their debts? Does the Chamber think it unjust to them that, in their turn, they were forced to send us back gold? It is from not looking at both sides of the case that confusion and false judgment arises. Every sound thinker will say that the foreigners acted honestly and honourably in sending us gold in payment of their balances. This gold was purchased by the Bank of England, and paid for in their notes. These, being needed for a now reviving domestic trade, were absorbed into the circulation of the country; prices gradually rose, and commercial prosperity returned.

Our non-commercial readers will perhaps understand the "currency question" better when we add a very simple illustration. The English sovereign contains a quantity of gold equal in value to that contained in a French Napoleon and a quarter, or 25 francs. When the Bank of England note is payable in gold on demand, the bankers and money-changers of France give 25 francs for every pound of the English note, and also for every pound of the circular notes of the London Bankers, used by travellers in paying their expenses abroad. But when the English bank note is not payable in gold, the traveller receives only 20, or 22, or 23 francs for his English pound, according to the extent of the demand for English notes in France with which to pay debts due by Frenchmen *in England*. As these notes will not serve the Frenchmen as means of paying their own debts in Germany or America, they will give less and less of their own currency for them, in proportion to their own diminishing need of them as means of buying in England.

While, on the other hand, the English bank note is payable in gold, this depreciation of it in France cannot take place; because the English merchants, instead of sending bank notes beyond the amount which the Frenchmen need for paying their debts in England, would draw gold from the Bank of England, and *send it* to France in liquidation of their debts; and as English gold is received at its full value all over the world, the Frenchmen would take it at its full value, rather than receive bank notes which they could use only in England, and which were altogether useless to them when they did not desire to purchase English goods. By no human contrivance can English bank notes be preserved equal in value to the metallic currencies of foreign nations, except by making them payable in gold on demand; and the moment the bank note is allowed to fall below the value of the foreign metallic currencies, every English merchant buying in foreign markets, and every English traveller spending his money abroad, sustains losses on his bank and circular notes, which are his instruments of payment, fluctuating with the extent of the purchases made by the country in which he happens to buy or to travel, in the markets of England. Thus, a twenty pound English bank note, which, in France or Belgium, if the people of these countries were buying freely in England, might be taken at 23 francs in the pound; in Italy, which was buying less, might be taken at only 20; and in Spain, which buys still more restrictedly from us, at 18 francs. This happened during the suspension of gold payments in the last French war, and would inevitably occur again were suspension resorted to now.

Suspension, therefore, can benefit those persons only who are in debt beyond the amount of their tangible capital, and those who have trusted them—and even this only temporarily, and always at the expense of prudent capitalists who are not submerged in debt, and whose interest it is to keep the English currency equal in value to that of every country in which they mean to buy or to travel.

(From the Scotsman of December 8, 1855.)

THE provisions of the Bank Restriction Act of 1844, and the causes of the present demand for gold, require a brief elucidation.

The currency question has been debated in Parliament and discussed in the press at intervals during the whole of this century. Under the pressure of the war with France, Parliament declared the Bank-of-England note a legal tender in payment of debt, and specie speedily disappeared from circulation. The Bank thus obtained power to increase and diminish the currency according to their own notions of expediency, unchecked by the obligation to pay gold. Under this system, the only restraint on the circulation of the country bankers, was the necessity of redeeming their own notes in Bank-of-England notes on demand. The country was flooded with paper-currency, which was issued and withdrawn as the occurrences of the war frightened or gave confidence to bankers; and price rose and fell with a rapidity and suddenness that defied all ordinary calculation. Trade became a species of gambling, and gold attained a maximum of $15\frac{1}{2}$ per cent. above the Mint price. Guineas at one time sold for 27s. in Bank-of-England notes; and foreign exchanges were ruinously adverse to England;

the exchange on Hamburgh and Amsterdam, for example, was depressed in the end of 1809 to from 16 to 20 per cent. below par—that is to say, an English merchant who owed four pounds sterling in Hamburgh was under the necessity of giving five pounds in Bank-of-England notes for gold equal to four sovereigns with which to discharge his debt.

In 1810, Parliament entered on the serious consideration of this evil; and appointed a " Bullion Committee," of which Mr. Francis Horner was the first chairman. The report was drawn up by him, Mr. Huskisson, and Mr. Henry Thornton. The committee reported " that there was an excess in the paper circulation, of which the most unequivocal symptoms were the high price of bullion, and, next to that, the low state of the continental exchange; and the cause of this excess was to be found in the suspension of cash payments; there being no adequate provision against such excess, except the convertibility of paper into specie." They recommended • " the repeal of the law suspending the cash payments of the Bank," but proposed to allow the Bank two years to provide for the change.

This wise measure was not carried into effect till 1819; but then cash payments were resumed, amidst loud cries of ruin from the whole debtor class of the community; landowners who were in debt swelling the chorus of complaint uttered by commercial debtors. And there was apparently hardship in the case. Many of the debtors had bought and borrowed bank notes worth only 15s. or 16s. in the pound compared with gold, and were required to pay in gold or in bank notes equal in value to gold; and thus had from 15 to 20 per cent. added to their obligations. But the debtor classes who had borrowed money equal to gold in value had gained as much when the bank note fell, and they could pay off 20s. borrowed in gold with a bank note worth only 15s. in gold, Moreover, the suspension of specie payments was originally fixed to terminate at a certain time after the declaration of peace. Every engagement, therefore, entered into in the interval, was made subject to this contingency; and no one had a right to complain when the contingency arrived. There was no remedy, besides, for the canker in the vitals of commerce, but to make the sacrifice, and return to a sound currency convertible into specie.

Whenever the speculative and over-ardent class of merchants and manufacturers, having exceeded their legitimate command of capital, had involved themselves and their creditors in difficulties, they continued, for many years, to blame the resumption of cash payments as the cause of their distress; but Parliament adhered steadily to the law; and in 1844, after great deliberation and discussion, the existing arrangements were adopted.

Mr. Jones Loyd, now Lord Overstone, writing in 1840, says:— " It is now discovered that there is a liability to excessive issues of paper, even while that paper is convertible at will;" and it was to prevent this evil that the Act of 1844 was passed.

The Government then ascertained the average amount of notes which every bank in the United Kingdom had been able to keep in circulation to answer the ordinary transactions of business during a certain period, and allowed them to continue to issue to that extent without giving any security beyond that which they had always given—viz., the security afforded by their capital and the universal liability of the partners for the debts of the bank. In England the country banks are limited to their ascertained average circulation, and any increased issue by them must be in gold, or Bank-of-England notes. But the Act allowed the Scotch banks to increase their issues on condition of holding gold equal to the excess of their circulation above the ascertained average. It also permitted the banks of Ireland to issue to their average amounts, as before the Act, but beyond these only to the extent of the gold held at the four head offices of each of the banks; what is held by the other branches not being included. By this means the temptation to excessive issues was withdrawn, because there was no profit from notes merely given in exchange for gold which lay unproductive in their vaults.

Before the date of the Act, the Bank-of-England had purchased fourteen millions of Government stocks, and paid for them in their own notes. It turned out on investigation, that these notes remained permanently in circulation. The Bank thus acquired the Government funds at the cost of the paper on which their notes were printed and the stamp duty: beyond this expense, and the charges incident to maintaining the notes in circulation, the dividends were clear gain. The Act allows this circulation to continue as long as the public chooses to use the notes; but it declares that the fourteen millions of stocks shall remain under pledge, as security to the public for payment of them. Although, in respect of this security, it does not *require* the Bank to hold gold in its vaults for these notes, it leaves the Bank's obligation to pay gold for them on demand unimpaired. On the other hand, in consideration of the advantages the Bank enjoys under this arrangement, it manages the National Debt and other national business on very low terms.

The obligation on the Bank-of-England to hold gold for their *surplus* issues above their authorised averages, was not fraught with any hardship or injustice to them; for when they purchased gold, they gave *only their own notes* in exchange for it, and these notes cost them only the price of the paper, printing, and stamp duty. As this is a view of the case not generally understood, we shall endeavour to elucidate it.

Suppose, then, that a merchant who had received a million in gold from Australia, in payment of goods which he had sent there, carried it to the Bank and offered it for sale, it is self-evident that he must have agreed to take their notes in exchange for it, because it would been sheer absurdity to exchange *his* gold for *their* gold. In this transaction, then, the bank notes are exactly equivalent to receipts in such terms as these:—"The Bank-of-England has received from Edward Thornton a deposit of one million of pounds sterling in gold, which it binds itself to restore to him, or the bearer of this receipt, on demand." The seller of the gold would use his bank notes in paying for more goods to be sent to Australiaor America; and the increase of manufacturing industry, and the buying and selling consequent on his purchases, would make the bank notes necessary *as currency* in settling these transactions. While this state of things continued, the gold would lie in the Bank, and the notes circulate in the country. Every fresh arrival of gold from abroad would be either a payment for goods already furnished, or a fund to be applied in purchasing more goods to be forwarded to the sender of the gold. It also would be carried to the Bank and exchanged for notes, and the trade excited by the purchases made with these notes would again absorb them into the general circulation.

During these transactions, gold would accumulate in the Bank; the circulation of notes would increase; and trade also would be extended in proportion to the purchases made. The gold would lie quietly in the vaults of the banks; and all that it would have cost them, as we have said, would be the expense of the notes promising to restore it on demand. To cover this, they give for gold a fraction less than the Mint price. Because large issues of bank notes are *concomitant* with commercial activity, many persons mistake the bank notes for the *cause* of the activity; whereas the *real cause* is the purchases made with the gold imported. In point of fact, the deposit of the gold in the banks' vaults, in exchange for their notes containing an obligation to restore it when demanded, is *an operation of mere convenience.* The notes are more manageable than gold in passing from hand to hand, and on this account alone are preferred, it being always certain that they are the real representatives of gold. A large accumulation of gold in the Bank, therefore, is simply accumulated payments by foreigners for the products of our industry which they have bought; and it *is these purchases* which have *caused* the activity of trade, and also, as *a concomitant*, a corresponding circulation of bank notes with which to carry on the transactions. In other words, the gold is an addition made to our *capital* engaged in trade; and every addition extends trade, as the abstraction of capital contracts it.

The cause of the gold coming here was, that foreigners had purchased, in our markets, more goods than they had sold to us—which turned the balance against them, and forced them to pay in gold. But, in the course of time, the tide again turns. The English people of all classes enriched by this active commerce, use large quantities of foreign produce for manufacturing and domestic purposes; while foreign merchants, being straitened at home, are necessitated to limit their orders for our goods. The balance, then, turns against us. Now, what do the Chamber recommend? Totally blind to the fact that the *cause* of the active commerce, and the large circulation of bank notes, was the extensive purchases by foreigners in our markets liquidated in gold, they desire, after these purchases have diminished—after the bank notes used in the trade which they had occasioned are returned upon the Bank, as no longer needed in circulation—and after the holders of the notes find it necessary to request the Bank to return the gold which was deposited when the notes were issued, that they may pay their own debts to foreigners with it—after all this, the Chamber desires that the Bank should not give back the gold represented by their notes, but that they should issue more notes, to be entangled in a commerce already so restricted in real transactions, as to be incapable of maintaining in circulation the notes previously issued! In England, bank notes never are returned extensively, accompanied with demands for gold, until a contraction has taken place in trade, which has rendered it incapable of maintaining them in circulation. The return of the notes to the Bank is merely a *symptom* of an already existing commercial collapse, and is not the *cause* of it. In such circumstances, to issue more notes, not payable in specie, or in anything else, would be a purely noxious absurdity.

In our next remarks we shall advert to the case of the Provincial Banks.

[*From the Scotsman of December* 12, 1855.]

IN our last article on the Currency, we stated that when the Bank of England buys gold, it pays for it in its own notes. We now add, that the English provincial banks also, so long as they keep within the limits of their authorised issues, buy gold and pay for it in their own notes, although not so directly as the Bank of England does. With their own notes they discount bills payable in London; send these to their London agents, who receive payment of them in Bank of England notes, with which they procure gold from the Bank, and send it to their constituents. In their case, also, the gold is held in deposit till the holders of their notes request them to pay it over to them; and they lose nothing except the cost of the paper and the printing of the notes, and the fraction of the stamp duty corresponding to the time during which the notes are in circulation: the double return, on capital and unsecured note circulation, enables them to bear this trifling expense. It is only when they issue beyond the amount of their authorised averages, that they must use gold or Bank of England notes, which they procure out of their capital; but this excess of issue is purely voluntary on their part, and if not profitable need not be made.

The Scotch Banks are included in the Act of 1844, and most of these observations apply to them. There are some peculiarities, however, in their circumstances, which require to be mentioned. The foreign trade of Scotland is adjusted chiefly through bills payable in London, and gold is scarcely ever demanded on a large scale from the Scotch Banks. Their notes are used as currency in settling domestic transactions, and, on certain days, are exchanged—that is to say, the notes issued by each bank are brought back to it by all the other banks into which they have been paid; balances are struck, and every debtor bank pays the balance which it owes to the creditor banks in Exchequer Bills, or in bills payable in London. Practically, this is equal to paying the balances in gold; for Exchequer Bills and London drafts can command gold in London whenever required. There is thus small inducement to the Scotch Banks to over-issue; and hence, in ordinary times, their circulation is regulated pretty closely to the amount of currency actually needed by the community for the purposes of trade. If, however, the obligation to pay their notes in gold, when demanded, were repealed, and if the over-issues of each bank were not payable in bills that could command gold, what check would remain on banks disposed to increase their circulation by reckless issues to foster speculative schemes? Under the Suspension Act in the French war, some Scotch Banks actually pursued this course, and the respectable banks refuse to receive their notes. The older members of the community will recollect the annoyance which this occasioned in trade, and the anxiety felt to get quit of the notes of these banks, as their failure was daily anticipated, and at last occurred.

As the banks are liable to a fine if their issues exceed the statutory amount of gold which the Act requires them to hold, they prudently keep in hand a stock in excess of their actual issues. This portion of gold must be paid for out of capital, and to that extent they lose the interest of it as an investment; but the precautionary surplus thus retained is rarely large; and, as it is discretionary, it should not be taken into account in a question relative to a sound and serviceable national currency.

Thus it appears, that when there is no panic about the solvency of banks, gold is never demanded on a large scale, except for exportation; for this simple reason, that the individuals who carry on the ordinary transactions of the country, absorb and retain in circulation a number of notes corresponding to their trade. Each of us has one, five, ten, twenty, or a hundred pounds in bank notes in his possession, for daily use; and the aggregate of these is the aggregate circulation authorised by the Act 1844 to be issued, the greater part of it, without being represented by gold. While the credit of the banks is undoubted, no one thinks of desiring gold for these notes, although the banks are bound to pay it when required. But a most certain way to destroy this confidence, is to increase the number of the notes beyond what is needed for the transactions of a healthy commerce. Once issue notes as currency to individuals who desire to extend their railroad shares, their mills, their machinery, their stocks in trade, faster than the growth of the wealth and numbers of the people require, and you introduce ruin. The things produced not being then needed, become unsaleable; production is suspended, and trade collapses. The notes issued to call the things into existence, cannot be kept in circulation when the buying and selling of them cease; and *traders never apply to bankers to take goods or other property, directly or indirectly, in pledge for notes, except when it is more advantageous to them to borrow upon, than to sell the things.* Their demand is, that the bankers should hold these goods for their benefit, till they become saleable. But what shall be done with the bank notes? There are no transactions going forward requiring them for circulation. They are, therefore, immediately paid back, as deposits or in payment of debts, to the bankers, who must retain them till a healthy trade arises. What merchant, for instance, keeps a hundred pounds of bank notes, needed in brisk times, constantly in his desk, when he finds that his transactions in buying and selling have diminished so much, that fifty pounds now suffice to accomplish them ? If he have confidence in his banker, he will send the other fifty pounds to him, to be placed to his credit, till better times arrive. If he doubts the banker's solvency, he will demand gold for them.

The Act of 1844 contains a provision for supplying, to the extent of two-thirds, any deficiency in the paper-currency that may arise through any banks privileged to issue notes ceasing to do so. At present, by the closing of certain banks, the paper-currency is diminished to the extent of £700,000 below the aggregate amount authorised in 1844. In this emergency, the Bank of England is authorised to supply the deficiency to the extent of two-thirds, or £470,000; but mark the conditions. It must deposit Consols or Exchequer Bills as securities for this amount; and the government draws the dividends and interest on them, less the expense estimated to be sustained in the manufacture of the notes, and the management of that portion of the circulation. The government here recognises the evil of allowing the double return of profit enjoyed by the provincial banks while permitted to receive—1st, the dividends arising from capital invested in profitable securities; and, 2nd, the interest of the notes issued on the faith of them.

A mystification has been raised about certain operations of the Bank of France in drawing gold from the Bank of England. The Bank of France discounted with its own notes acceptances payable in London by English merchants to Frenchmen, wherever it could find them; sent these to London, and re-discounted them there for English bank notes; drew gold from the Bank for the amount, and carried it to Paris. This is said to be an exceptional transaction—one not likely to occur again—and so forth. But let us put it to the test. English acceptances could not exist in France unless Englishmen had bought in French markets. At the end of sixty, ninety, or a few more days, they would be payable in London at maturity. The Bank of France may have anticipated by these days the date when the French holders were entitled to demand, and the English acceptors bound to make payment of them in gold, or in notes convertible into gold. This is the sum and substance of the operation. But, on the other hand, if French merchants had bought to equal amounts in England, and granted acceptances payable in Paris, the Bank of England might have sought for and discounted these in London, sent them to Paris, re-discounted them for notes of the Bank of France, demanded gold for the notes, and brought it back to their own vaults. If they did not think it expedient to do this, then what would ensue? The French acceptances would fall due in a brief space of time; the Parisian merchants would pay them in notes of the Bank of France or in gold. If paid in notes, and if, by the previous proceedings of the Bank of France, the rate of exchange had been turned against Paris, the correspondents of the London houses would certainly draw gold for them and send it to England.

We shall take leave of the subject in a very few further remarks, which, however, we think it better to give in a short concluding article.

[*From the Scotsman of December* 15, 1855.]

FOR the reasons stated in our last article on the currency, it is highly improbable that gold should be drawn from the Bank of England for exportation, unless England is in debt to foreign nations. And there is no mystery in the present drain upon the Bank. England has purchased largely in foreign markets; she has a large army on foot, and two large fleets afloat, supplied more or less by foreigners with things necessary for their use; she has subscribed to a Turkish loan of five millions, and to a Sardinian loan of one million, and from all these causes she is in debt to foreigners; and she is bound to send gold in extinction of her obligations, cost what it will.

The war is at present highly popular, and we do not utter a word against it; but we must screw up our courage to encounter its consequences. We are spending large amounts of capital in it, which are withdrawn from manufacturers and commerce; and as these cannot safely or permanently extend beyond the limits of the capital which sustains them, collapse in trade is the inevitable temporary result of our war expenditure. This expenditure by England in foreign loans and in maintaining fleets and armies abroad, must be provided for; and there is no provision that will suffice but to export our own produce to an equal amount, or to pay in gold. It depends on the will of foreigners whether they will take our goods or not, and *when*; and a demand on the Bank of England for gold is simply a proof that *at present* they are not purchasing commodities from us to an amount equal to our debts to them. The Bank has no alternative but to furnish gold and to contract the circulation, and thereby to deprive our merchants of the means of spending more money abroad, and also to cause such a fall in our home prices as will tempt foreigners to renew their purchases and send back the gold to us. This will happen, sooner or later; meantime, our present embarrassments are the price we are paying for the war and for the foreign produce which we have consumed beyond the value of the goods which we have sold.

We must here advert to an argument on which the opponents of a convertible currency place great reliance. They say, What we desire is, a currency for home circulation which shall be adequate to the wants of trade, leaving the merchants who deal with foreigners to buy gold like any other commodity, when they need it, to pay their debts abroad. But the difficulty lies here. If the home currency is not by law convertible into gold, it may be issued to such excess (as was the case in the French war) that the merchants may be compelled to give five pounds in it for gold equal to four sovereigns; and who can estimate the extent of derangement that would then ensue in our foreign trade? The price of gold purchased as a commodity with inconvertible domestic currency, would vary with the ever-changing quantities of that currency issued; and in one month the merchant might obtain gold equal to four sovereigns for £4 10s., in another month for £4 15s., and in a third only for £5. No man, when he ordered any article from abroad, could calculate the sum which he would be forced to pay for it in domestic currency when it arrived; for the price of the gold in which he must pay it would fluctuate with the quantity of that currency *then* in circulation. The Act of 1844 effectually saves merchants dealing with foreign countries from this evil; because it preserves the domestic currency always equal in value to gold, and places it in their power to convert it into sovereigns or bullion without loss or delay.

It is absurd also to attempt to separate our domestic from our foreign trade, and to propose to carry them on by means of different currencies. No nation in the world is so dependent on its foreign trade as Great Britain. Look at the enormous extent of our annual exports and imports, and consider the consequences of deranging the settlement of all these transactions by adopting a domestic currency fluctuating in value in relation to gold so much that no man could calculate the prices of these articles in that currency a week before the day of settlement. Our domestic trade is based on our foreign traffic, and could not flourish under its embarrassment. No one who recollects the state of our home markets during the years of suspension in the French war, and recalls the reckless speculations, the innumerable bankruptcies, the sudden and uncontrollable rise and fall of private fortunes, the broken hearts, the destitution of families, and the innumerable other evils which accompanied that suspension, will ever desire to see such days return.

Another argument frequently used by the opponents is—" Let us have free trade in currency, as in everything else." Be it so, and what then? We must begin by repealing the act establishing a legal tender for debt, and allow every man to issue currency, and every other person to accept or reject it, when tendered as payment, as he pleases. Then, in every transaction, each of us must bargain, not only about the quantity and quality of the article, *but also about the currency in which it shall be paid*; and what would be the condition of trade under such a system? Let the opponents answer this question; or reconcile the existence of a legal tender, which necessarily implies the exclusion of all other things as standards, with perfect freedom to every one to issue his own currency, and to offer it to the public as a standard at his discretion.

In the preceding remarks, we do not maintain that all the details of the Act of 1844 are perfect; some of these may require to be modified to suit the changes in the wealth and population of the country since that date; and experience may have shown how others can be improved. All we contend for is a currency convertible into gold on demand ; and that the convertibility shall be real and direct, and not a sham. To render convertibility *real*, we hold that *there must be restriction* on the issue of paper-currency. In 1840, Lord Overstone showed that the mere promise by bankers to pay gold on demand afforded no adequate guarantee for their being actually able to do so; and in his speech on the Bill of 1844, Sir Robert Peel demonstrated this fact by proofs unanswerable. It is an open question *how* the restriction may be imposed with the least inconvenience and the greatest advantages; but we repeat that, in our judgment, restriction is indispensable to ensure real convertibility.

The present clamourers for suspension carefully conceal the facts that every commercial convulsion that has occurred since the resumption of cash payments in 1819, was preceded by two or three years of speculative excitement and over-trading ; and that the great sufferers were the imprudent persons who had engaged in these transactions, and their creditors. Their Magnus Apollo, Malachi Malagrowther, is an example of the class. Not satisfied with the large gains acquired by his splendid talents, he bought land, built a miniature baronial castle, and became bookseller and publisher, chiefly on borrowed money ; and when the banks declined to continue his supply of currency, he was forced to suspend payments himself. What the opponents of the Bank Restriction Act appear to us to require is, a currency that shall give ardent men, who have little or no capital, a supply of it on easy terms ; a currency, moreover, possessed of the magic virtue of fostering production, and yet rendering over-production impossible: of enabling men to speculate rashly, and yet saving them from the consequences of miscalculation; a currency, in short, which shall enable them to disregard the laws appointed by Providence to regulate human transactions, and still preserve to them all the prosperity which Divine Wisdom attaches to the observance of these laws. When the Chamber of Commerce and Mr. J. F. Macfarlan shall enable Parliament to furnish such a currency, we shall hail then as beings greater than men.

————

[*From the Scotsman of December* 22, 1855.]

In another column we have published a letter from Mr. W. Little on the Currency,* in which he approves of bank notes being made payable in gold on demand, but maintains that, " in place of the present system of centralisation, we want full and free competition all over the kingdom among bankers and money-lenders. With perfect freedom and action, all evils will finally correct and adjust themselves. Who can be so able to regulate the extent of liability or credit between lenders and borrowers as the person directly interested ? . . . . . If I prefer the security of a single person or

* See Appendix.

private bank to that of a joint-stock association, where the directors, with the whole mass of shareholders, are liable for the repayment of my deposits, that must be my own affair, and I alone must be responsible for the result." So far as we are aware, no one proposes to limit the competition of bankers, or to interpose between them and their depositors and borrowing customers; but under the foregoing phraseology, Mr. Little appears in reality to object to any restriction on the number of notes which bankers may issue, provided they bear on the face of them the words, " I promise to pay five pounds," or any other sum. He, and many other persons, appear to consider the obligation to pay gold on demand all that is needed for the public safety, and that every one may be left to judge for himself of the bankers' *ability* to fulfil his promise. But this opinion is contradicted by all experience. From 1819 to 1844, this was the state of the law. The Bank of England was bound to pay its notes in gold, and the provincial banks were bound to pay in gold or Bank of England notes; and the public was left at liberty to judge for themselves of the ability of each bank to redeem its issue. And what was the consequence ? In prosperous times, everybody believed in the ability of every bank to redeem on demand, and the country was flooded with bank notes. In 1837, when a crash occurred in the United States, which diminished our exports, and involved many of our merchants and manufacturers in ruin, it became necessary to export gold in payment of our debts; the Bank of England gave up its treasures on demand, but, to prevent its own suspension, it did not re-issue the notes retired for gold. This deprived the provincial bankers of a command of Bank of England notes ; and, as they had never thought of providing themselves with gold sufficient to retire their own notes, when the public became alarmed, and rushed to their counters and demanded Bank of England notes or gold, they shut their doors and suspended payments. The number of banks which failed at this time was so great as to spread desolation over the land. And have we in Scotland, with all our individual sharpness and caution, and our admirable system of banking, never taken bank notes which the issures of them were unable to redeem? Have we forgotten the failure of Maberly and Co., the Leith Bank, the Renfrewshire Bank, the East Lothian Bank, the Fife Banking Company, the Montrose Bank, the Stirling Bank ?

It is no answer to say that the notes of several of these banks were ultimately redeemed out of the private estates of the partners —for this was effected only after years of delay, the payments being made by instalments at long intervals as the funds were collected ; and surely a currency of this sort is a public nuisance, although it may be ultimately redeemed. We may safely permit buyers and sellers, and lenders and borrowers, to judge of each other's solvency; but issuing paper currency is neither buying nor selling, nor simply lending or borrowing. It begins indeed by lending bank notes to customers borrowing; but the transaction does not end there. The borrowers present the notes to the public, and ask them to receive and pass them from hand to hand as equivalent to gold ; and the public, many of whom are working men, professional men, agriculturists, and women, have no adequate means of judging whether they are equal in value to gold or not. Parliament, therefore, which allows the notes to be issued, is bound to help these classes, and all others of limited knowledge in this emergency ; and to place such restrictions on the issues as shall give them a reasonable security that the notes shall be redeemed. The Bank Restriction Act contains the best regulations for accomplishing this end which we have yet seen proposed.

Our American brethren have tried the experiment of unrestricted issues also. They make bank notes payable in specie, but leave each individual to receive or reject them as currency at his discretion ; and what is the result ? Any reader of the *New York Journal of Commerce*, or other American commercial newspapers, will find a list of bank notes in actual circulation in currency, printed in small type, and a foot or a foot and a half long, specifying the actual special value of the notes of each bank in the State ; and the values run from par to $\frac{1}{4}$, $\frac{1}{2}$, $\frac{3}{4}$, or 1 per cent. discount, to 5 or 10 per cent. discount, according to the credit of the bank ! It is as difficult to master the specie value of the notes of all the banks in a State, so as to be able safely to buy and sell with them, as to learn a science ! And people are forced to carry these lists in their pockets, and consult them when unknown notes are presented to them. This is felt to be so great a nuisance, and such innumerable bank failures occur in these States, that their legislators have resorted to every possible mode of imposing *indirect* restrictions on issues. For example :—The law requires all duties on articles imported (and these constitute the chief revenue of the United States' general government), to be paid in specie. This forces the bankers at the seaports constantly to hold a stock of gold, and also to limit their issues, so as to preserve a safe proportion between the specie in their vaults and their notes in circulation. In the State of New York, the banks are required also to publish their circulation, deposits, discounts, and loans, and stock of gold weekly ; and any errors in their statements, which ordinary care might have enabled them to avoid, are declared to subject the bank officers to imprisonment for a period of years in the State prison ! Moreover, the banks are prohibited from making a dividend beyond the amount of profit actually realised in the year, under the same penalty. Experience has led the freest, the most acute, the keenest and most enterprising people on earth to resort to these indirect means of placing " restrictions " on bank note issues—and shall this experience be lost on us ?*

* The privilege of issuing Bank notes based on securities, and promising to pay specie on demand, was left to the Americans *without any restriction ;* and the precautions mentioned in the text, aided by all previous experience, have proved insufficient to prevent such an excess of issues as to render payment in specie *impossible.* In consequence, the whole currency of the United States has collapsed, all the Banks have suspended cash payments, the exchanges, foreign and domestic, are deranged, and the commercial public of the

The opponents of the Bank Restriction Act, who represent the contraction of bank note circulation as the *cause,* instead of the effect, of their embarrassments, clamour for extension of paper issues in proportion to the efflux of gold. If this were a sound and serviceable remedy for their evils, certainly the acute Americans, who have no Bank Restriction Act like ours, would have found out the fact and practised on it ; yet hear the advice given in the "money article" of the *New York Herald,* of 28th November, 1855, to the merchants of that city, who are in monetary difficulties, occasioned by the contraction of their credits in England, and other causes. Our Chamber of Commerce, in such a case, would probably say: " Never mind the foreigners, let us look to ourselves— issue more bank notes, and keep the currency full ;" but not so writes the *Herald.* It says :—

" We have not merely our local affairs to look to in the present emergency. We cannot trust to our internal resources to extricate ourselves from financial difficulties, in the event of our European creditors demanding large payments. We must, before the avalanche of our stock securities comes upon us, prepare ourselves for it by the *contraction* in all our domestic credits. We must provide ourselves available means to meet any foreign demand that may arise, by the sale in our markets of our own stocks, for foreign account ; *and we must by contraction of credits, reduce prices so that our export trade will become more active, and our import trade more restricted.* The financial policy of Great Britain is at present just this and no more. Any advance in the rate of interest by the Bank of England, produces a contraction in commercial transactions, reduces prices at home, gives a great impetus to the export trade, and ultimately turns the current of specie from all parts of the world into the ports of the United Kingdom. These things operate actively, and soon the required result appears in all the channels of commerce. To counteract the effect of such a policy on the part of England, we are forced into the same system. To prevent our markets from being flooded with foreign manufactures—to prevent our banks from being drained of gold—to prevent, if possible, the return of our securities in large amounts—we must restrict credits and commercial transactions, and that can only be done by a contraction of bank loans. We have not an interest sliding-scale, and must therefore apply the remedy at once directly to the root of the evil. If the pursuance of this stringent policy ; if, in destroying markets for foreign manufactures, we reduce prices for our own products, it must be considered as only partial evil for universal good ; *for the very fact of reducing prices for our staple products would give such an impetus to exports as would at once remove all apprehensions of further shipments of specie."*

This is simply a recognition of the law which everywhere controls the transactions of commerce, and from which no nation can emancipate itself by artificial devices.

[*From the Scotsman of February 14, 1856.*]

In another column we have inserted a letter from Mr. W. Little on the Bank Restriction Act, which he promises shall be his last. In making a few observations on it, we hope that we shall be spared the necessity of reverting to the subject, at least until it come before Parliament in a substantive form.

Union are now, (Dec., 1857), suffering under a severe monetary convulsion. See article from *Scotsman* of 30th November, 1857, p. 36.

Mr. Little, in common with many other persons, assumes that the great object of the Bank Restriction Act of 1844 was to prevent commercial convulsions; but this is a mistake. Sir Robert Peel, it is true, stated that this was *one* of its objects; but its main design was to ensure the instantaneous conversion of bank notes into gold on demand, and thereby to avert the panics which occurred when the failure of several banks to redeem their notes excited suspicion of the solidity of all, and caused a sudden and general run upon them for specie. The holders of the notes of suspended banks found them no more useful as currency, with which to pay their own debts or to make purchases, than waste paper; and great inconvenience, and in many instances heavy losses, were sustained by the assets of the banks ultimately falling short of their obligations. The Act of 1844 has had the effect of preventing, to a remarkable extent, the recurrence of this evil, as we shall presently show.

Mr. Little maintains that the obligation to pay gold on demand is all that is required to ensure actual conversion, and that the public may be safely left to judge for themselves of the *ability* for every bank of issue to redeem its notes. As this assertion bears directly on the merits of the Act of 1844, we shall appeal to a few well-known facts, and leave our readers to form their own judgment of its truth.

On 12th December, 1825, the banking-house of Sir Peter Pole and Co., who acted as agents in London for forty-four English provincial banks, suspended payment, and within six weeks, seventy provincial banks closed their doors in insolvency. Their failure caused a panic and a general run upon the still solvent banks; and although many of these maintained their ground, they did so only by enormous sacrifices of their property, while others fell before the storm. Desolation and alarm spread over all ranks in almost every country in England. Here, then, the obligation to pay in gold, implicitly relied on by the public, was found insufficient to ensure its due fulfilment in the hour of trial. With a view to avert these catastrophes, and especially to protect the working-classes from loss by the non-redemption of one-pound notes, which circulated largely among them, Parliament prohibited the issue of any bank notes below £5 after the 5th April 1829, and it also legalised the establishment of joint-stock banks in the provinces, with universal liability on all the partners for their debts.

These measures produced a partial effect in securing the convertibility of bank notes; but again a great speculative excitement seized the nation, and in 1836 between two and three hundred joint-stock companies, including banks and railroads, were started. In 1838, the crop of grain was very deficient in the United Kingdom, which led to very large importations of corn. At the same time, many of the wild speculations of the previous years had come to a close in disaster and ruin. A collapse of trade, shaking of credit, and a large export of gold simultaneously took place; and in 1839 another flood of bankruptcy and suffering desolated the country. Again a number of banks failed, affording additional evidence that the mere obligation to pay gold on demand does not suffice to ensure the actual conversion of the bank note when the day of pressure unexpectedly arrives.

The leading objects of the Act of 1844 were to increase the public security that bank notes should be actually redeemed on demand, and to afford means by which prudent persons of all classes might descry the approach of a money pressure, and prepare for it by contracting in due season their credits and obligations. It aimed at accomplishing the first object by restricting the circulation of bank notes, as formerly explained; and the second by the publication of the monetary condition of the Bank of England. The diminution of the stocks of gold and reserve notes in the Bank indicates a contraction of the sources from which loans and discounts are supplied to the commercial classes as certainly as a fall in the barometer intimates the approach of a disturbance of the atmosphere at sea. We appeal with confidence to persons who have had the best means of observing the varying phases of commerce, whether, comparing the bank failures during the period from 1819, when convertibility was enforced by law, to 1844, with those that have occurred from 1844 to the present time, there has not been a great diminution of these catastrophes in the latter period. Moreover, since 1844 the bank note and sovereign have been kept steadily of equal value, so that the English merchant, desiring to discharge a debt due by him, or to make a purchase in Hamburgh, Leghorn, or New York, when the rate of exchange was against England, instead of being forced, as in former days, to pay five pounds in bank notes for gold equal to four sovereigns, has always been able to pay his foreign debts without loss, if he held bank notes in his possession, or had a balance in his favour with his bankers. These certainly are no trifling advantages gained by means of the Act of 1844, and even its opponents acknowledge that it has conferred the latter benefit. The author of " Currency, Self-Regulating and Elastic," admits that " the object of making the currency contract and expand exactly as a metallic one would do, may be said to have been attained," although he denies its efficacy in preventing convulsions.—p. 263.

Mr. Little concurs in this objection, and maintains that commercial convulsions arise from abuse of credit, and that the contraction or expansion of the currency has no influence on credit. We agree with him in ascribing the root of collapses in trade and insolvency of debtors to an unwise extension of credit, and admit, also, that the Act of 1844 does not, and never was expected by those who understand its provisions, to supersede the exercise of judgment and discretion on the part of bankers in giving credit. The means in the hands of a bank of issue applicable to lending and discounting are—1st. Its capital; 2ndly. The money entrusted to it as deposits; and 3rdly. Its own notes. The only portions of these which the directors may dispose of absolutely at discretion is their own capital. They are liable at any moment to be called on to pay up the deposits, and to redeem their notes in gold. Experience shows, indeed, that in ordinary times, and while the stability of a bank is undoubted, a certain amount of the deposits will remain permanently in its possession, and a certain amount of its notes permanently in circulation; and to such extents loans from these sources may, *in ordinary times*, be safely made to its customers. In dull times, following a commercial crisis, production is limited, small stocks of goods are held, and credit is sparingly given; in consequence of which much capital, usually invested in trade, is set free from its form of commodities, and assumes that of money. The owners of it, still trembling at recent losses, are averse to risk it in new investments, and lodge it with their bankers as deposits. It accumulates in their hands to large amounts, and they find it difficult to obtain employment for it, on which their profit depends. This was the state of things for some time prior to 1847. Money was lying idle, and to induce its customers to use it, the Bank of England lowered the rate of discount and of interest on loans. Other banks followed in their wake, and they soon found ardent and hopeful men ready to accept of their aid, and to borrow as fast as they were willing to lend. The money, put into the hands of these customers, was speedily reconverted into goods, houses, mills, railroads, and other forms of corporeal embodiment, and this was called a revival of trade and renewal of prosperity.

For a time every undertaking appeared to flourish—interest was low, " money was easy," prices rose, and people believed themselves becoming rapidly rich. At length, however, the cautious depositors, whose money, lent by the banks, partly supplied the stimulus to these new speculations, were drawn into the current: they called up their deposits, and invested them in the favourite speculations of the day. Merchants, also, bought largely in foreign markets, and the balance was turned against England. A deficient harvest in this country, and a short crop of cotton in America, completed the mischief. A drain commenced on the Bank of England for gold to pay debts abroad. This was the beginning of a new convulsion. The deposits being diminished, and the circulating notes returned for gold, two great sources of loans and discounts were dried up, and the banks, in general, had no alternative but to call in their loans, limit their discounts, and thus contract credit at its source. These operations were speedily followed by contraction of loans, discounts, and credits in all the branch streams of commerce into which the now abstracted money had flowed. Prices fell; and traders, who were in debt, and whose stock, estimated at the diminished prices, fell short of their obligations, became insolvent. The directors of the Bank of England, by mistakes committed in their banking department, aggravated the ultimate pressure; but the Act of 1844 arrested them, and preserved the convertibility of their notes.

It is obvious that no legislation can provide protection against such events. The only safeguard that will be effectual must be looked for in a higher intelligence and morality in our trading people, bankers included. The maxim that self-interest, acting in the spirit of its own blind intuitions, will certainly find its way to success, without troubling itself to observe the natural laws which regulate the production and distribution of wealth, must be exploded, and wiser courses followed : meantime, the question remains whether an unlimited power of issuing bank notes, if nominally payable in gold, has the effect of enabling banks to extend credit or not. Mr. Little maintains that it has not ; but we must postpone the consideration of this point till another opportunity.

[*From the Scotsman of February* 19, 1856.]

IN our paper of the 14th February, we mentioned that Mr. Little maintains that an unlimited power of issuing notes, if payable in gold, does not enable banks to increase credit, " because," says he, " banks cannot increase their circulation beyond the wants of the public; and whenever they exceed these limits, their notes are immediately returned to them." It is quite true that banks cannot themselves extend their circulation at pleasure, but by the aid of their customers they may do so, as far as the latter have the capacity to employ the notes in buying, building, improving, enlarging, etc. ; and while confidence is unshaken, we know no limits to such evolutions. If currency notes be one of the means by which bankers are enabled to furnish loans and discounts, it is pretty evident that, while customers are willing to borrow—if the supply of these notes be unlimited—the power of lending must be equally extensive. We are speaking chiefly of England, because the Scotch system of exchange, formerly explained, furnishes a valuable check against over-issues, at least on the part of individual banks. When the deposits are called up, the bankers pay them off in their own notes; and when bills are presented for discount, they give their own notes in exchange for them. These notes must either continue to circulate as currency, or be returned to the banks in payment of debts or as fresh deposits ; and while confidence is entire and discretion asleep, there appears no limit to the extent of credit, and of speculation based on credit, which such a system may engender. But a time comes when a demand for gold for exportation, and the exaggerated extent of speculative transactions, excite alarm ; nobody will now lend, while every creditor presses his debtors for payment. Suspicion attaches to the banks, and a run upon them commences for gold, which they cannot pay ; and the public then discovers that bank notes are not money, but only its representatives—that *confidence* is not *security*—and that excessive liberality in loans and discounts with depositors' funds and bank notes is neither wise in banks nor beneficial to traders.

It seems to us vain, therefore, to maintain that the legislative restriction of bank notes to that amount which experience shows corresponds to the healthy and normal transactions of the community is not, so far as these notes are sources of credit, a safeguard against excessive and indiscreet loans and discounts, which, as already remarked, lay the foundations of excessive credits, and end in panics and commercial convulsions.

We do not enter into Mr. Little's statistics, because the notecirculation of the Bank of England is only one of its sources of credit, and he has not given us an account of its deposits. Moreover, he is not very exact in his reading of his own figures. He says that "from February 1844 to August 1847, the circulation remained constant." But his table shows that in August, 1844, the circulation was £21,148,000, and that in August, 1847, it was £18,485,000—showing a contraction to the extent of £2,663,000, or more than 12 per cent.; the effect of which, as the value of everything is affected by the quantity of currency afloat, would be very perceptible in lowering prices and circumscribing credit. Besides, we have acknowledged that the directors of the Bank of England committed great errors as bankers for some time previous to 1847. They lent their deposits and extended their circulation too largely, and by low rates of interest fostered speculation. The Act of 1844 could not control their use either of their own capital or deposits, but, as already mentioned, it arrested them in their course, and preserved the convertibility of their notes. The bullion in 1847 never fell below £8,312,691.

Mr. Little is of opinion that the experience of bankers and merchants in the United States is not applicable as a guide to conduct in England, because the circumstances of the two countries are different. On the contrary, we are persuaded that the laws which regulate the production and distribution of wealth are based in Nature, and are universal in their operation, and that money and banking are merely instruments for facilitating production and distribution, and are as thoroughly subject to the same laws as the motions of a satellite are to those of the principal planet. In the State of New York there is no Bank Restriction Act, and nevertheless, the bankers of the city of New York act on the principles we have so strenuously maintained. The money article of the *New York Herald* for January 1, 1856, contains the following remarks. They are long but very instructive:—

"A large amount of money belonging to regular merchants, which had accumulated in our banks as deposits, found its way into fancy stocks, and so long as that money remained in those securities, prices kept up; but as soon as its withdrawal commenced, those stocks accumulated in the street, and the market value ran rapidly down. About the middle of September the banks commenced contracting. The drain of specie for exportation, the news from Europe relative to the war, the indications of a severe financial stringency throughout Europe, created considerable alarm among our bank managers, and a rapid reduction in loans took place. This compelled large sales of stock securities, and prices ran down fast. At this time the demand upon the banks from their regular customers—from the mercantile classes—was very great, while the weekly returns exhibited a steady reduction in discounts. Call loans made on the hypothecation of stocks were demanded and paid at great sacrifices. The merchants were hard pressed for money, and stocks were thrown upon the market in large lots . . . . About the middle of O tober our financial and commercial advices from England were anything but satisfactory . . . A stringency in the European money markets created a temporary panic among our financiers and speculators, and large lots of stock were forced off at very low prices. Some of the best securities in the market were unwarrantably depressed, and serious sacrifices were submitted to. A fall of ten and fifteen per cent. was realised in as many days, and numerous failures occurred among large holders. During this panic the banks continued contracting, and early in November the lowest point of loans was upwards of nine millions of dollars less than on the second week in August. In the same time the specie on hand had decreased about four millions of dollars. The banks could not supply the demand upon them for discounts, and money became very scarce. This continued throughout November, and with it a very dull stock market. Speculation disappeared. Outsiders had as much as they could do in providing for their legitimate wants, and abandoned Wall Street entirely. Fancy stocks settled down at low prices in the hands of operators for a rise, and after a time the market became steady. In November the shipments of specie were not large. The rapid decrease in exportations of bullion had a favourable effect upon our money markets, but did not change the policy of the banks. The amount of specie in the banks did not increase, and their line of loans remained unchanged........The month of December has been, on the whole, very quiet and very steady. Quotations for stocks have not varied much, and there has been no speculative movement of consequence. Prices have been well sustained; and at the close, those current compare very favourably with those ruling at the commencement."

Here the principles are clearly announced and practically acted on, that it is necessary to the welfare equally of banks and their customers, that bank-notes should not be permitted to sink in value below the of the currency of other countries using specie as their standard; that certain and immediate convertibility alone can maintain the bank note equal in value to specie; and that, in certain circumstances, contraction of issues is indispensable to maintain this convertibility, and is, therefore, called for by the best interests of the community.

NOTE REFERRED TO ON PAGE 11.

The State of Pennsylvania never *repudiated* its debts, as the Rev. Sydney Smith led England to believe. The governor and legislature in every session officially acknowledged the subsistence of the State's obligations, and promised to discharge them. The cause of the suspension of dividends was the *physical* impossibility experienced in collecting the taxes. In some of the country districts, no accredited currency existed. Reapers and labourers were paid by the farmers in wheat, pork, butter, eggs, and other produce; which they exchanged in the villages for tea, sugar, shoes, and other necessary articles. The farmers offered to pay their taxes also in produce; but the collectors could not add the function of provision-merchants to their official duties, and for some time the collection was suspended. As soon, however, as a sound currency was re-established, payment of taxes, and also of dividends on the State debts, was resumed. The arrears of the dividends were capitalised, and converted into new stock, bearing interest.

COMMENTS UPON THE PRESENT SUSPENSION OF THE BANK-CHARTER ACT.
From the Scotsman of 30th Nov. 1857.

In endeavouring to explain the effects produced by the Bank Restriction Act of 1844, we solicit attention to two simple propositions. A Bank of England note for £1000, while *unissued*, is merely a piece of paper — but when issued it is in law equivalent to a transfer, to that extent of gold, or government securities, from the Bank to the holder of the note. In the hands of the holder it then becomes *capital;* as much so, as a bar of gold of equal value would be. But in these forms, the bank note and gold cannot be conveniently use as *currency* in the ordinary operations of trade, such as paying wages, liquidating shop accounts, and retiring bills of exchange of ordinary amounts. While held in these forms, they are capital; which, however, can be converted into currency by sending the gold to the mint to be coined into a thousand sovereigns, and the note to the Bank of England to be exchanged for specie or for notes of a smaller denomination.

As formerly explained, in the United States there has been no legal limit to the multiplication of bank-notes. In that country, every one who could pledge stocks and property with a public officer enjoyed the privilege of issuing paper which served him at once as *capital* and *currency.* It enabled him to buy, to build, and to manufacture, as if it had been gold. In this country, we were not permitted by law to create *paper currency* at pleasure, and make it serve for the time as capital; and what have been the consequences of these different systems? In the United States, the unlimited additions to bank-notes, which served at once as capital and currency, stimulated production and consumption to prodigal excess, and the people generally fell into debt. If the currency had consisted exclusively of gold, and of bank-notes that were really convertible into gold, the speculators who had called into existence things far exceeding in quantity the wants of the community, and in consequence had run into debt beyond their means of paying, might have become bankrupt, and much loss might have been sustained; but the operations of commerce would not, for an hour, have been interrupted for want of *currency* with which to carry them on. The merchant in Missouri who was solvent and had a balance in his bank, if he was indebted to New York, could have had no difficulty, while the Missouri bank paid gold for its notes, in making a remittance to his creditor in liquidation of his debt. But when bank-notes had been multiplied to an extent that rendered their conversion into gold on demand *physically impossible,* and their inconvertibility caused them, although secured by pledged property, to be rejected as *currency* in distant States, and by foreign nations, then, even solvent merchants who held these notes and could not obtain for them the gold which the banks had promised to pay on demand, found it impossible to fulfil their distant engagements.

From the moment when bank-notes ceased to serve *everywhere as currency,* it became necessary to pay 105 or 110 dollars in the bank-notes of one city for 100 dollars in gold, with which to discharge a debt due in another distant town; the rate of depreciation in the notes varying according to the extent to which the people of the district had run into debt to distant creditors, and to the amount of the notes issued by their banks.

This state of things obstructed and deranged the ordinary operations of commerce in two ways; — *first*, it introduced an arbitrary and varying standard of value by which to measure prices — for example, a barrel of flour might be quoted at 5 dollars in Cincinnati currency, but this did not indicate its price in Missouri or New York currency; *secondly*, it became *impossible* to buy goods and to pay debts in distant places — because, for example, the bank-notes of Cincinnati not being accepted as currency in New-York, and the holder of these notes not being able to obtain specie for them from the banks, his business was completely paralysed. This is no fancy picture. We read in the American newspapers of November 1857, that in consequence of nearly universal Bank suspensions over the Union (the Atlantic cities included); the merchants of New York and Boston have been forced to desire their western debtors to send them wheat, or pork, or wine, or any other marketable article of produce, which they may sell, or ship to Europe; and thus they settle accounts.

This was the first effect of bank suspension. But, *secondly*, de positors found that, for the sums they had lodged with the banks, they could now obtain only inconvertible paper, which had fallen to a discount of 5, 10, or 20 per cent. in relation to specie; and the difference was to them sheer loss.

These, then, are the result of an *unrestricted* issue of bank-notes based on securities, and bearing a promise to pay specie on demand. By their mere excessive multiplication, these notes have, *first*, led the people into the wildest schemes of production and waste, and substituted, for an expected harvest of inordinate wealth, wide-spread bankruptcy and ruin — and, *secondly*, by their incapacity to serve as as currency, they have actually obstructed the common operations of commerce.

Has anything like this happened in England, since restrictions were imposed on the issue of bank-notes by the Act of 1844? No — our currency has never for a day been inconvertible. A debtor in Connemara, and one in John o'Groat's, who have current bank-notes, find no difficulty in making purchases and paying debts in Dublin, Glasgow, Edinburgh, or London. Prices of commodities in every market are quoted in a currency which is of the same value all over the United Kingdom, and a London corn merchant is not puzzled to discover what a quarter of wheat quoted at 60s. in the Haddington market, will cost him when paid in the currency of East-Lothian. Much less have our metropolitan merchants, through want of currency, been driven to the necessity of desiring their provincial debtors to remit the sums due to them in cattle, potatoes, oats, or broadcloth.

Let us open our understandings, then, to what the Bank Restriction Act was intended to do; and let us decide, on calm reflection, whether it has proved a failure in preserving to us, through all our perils, the inestimable advantage of a really convertible, and therefore serviceable, *currency*. To us it appears undeniably to have succeeded in doing so. But we admit, that it has not done another thing which it was never calculated to achieve — namely, to supply speculators with *capital* on easy terms under the name of currency.

The omission to keep in view the double function performed by gold and convertible bank-notes, when issued by a solvent bank, of serving at once as *capital* and *currency* has led the public mind into inextricable confusion on the subject of restriction, of which the advocates of unrestricted issues have largely availed themselves. The mystery may be cleared up by calling the managers and directors of the Western and City of Glasgow Banks, and others in similar circumstances, and the insolvent merchants to whom they have advanced the capital and deposits of their confiding customers, before a Committee of the House of Commons, and examining them as to the causes of the present commercial embarrassments. Let the merchants be asked — When you had funds of your own in any of the banks of your district, did you find a difficulty in obtaining *currency* with which to conduct your exchanges, both at home and abroad? They could give only one answer — "No." Let the next question be — "When you extended your transactions beyond the limits of your own resources, was it *currency* as a medium of exchange that you wanted,

or *capital?*" Only one answer could be returned to this question—
"It was capital." Then let them be asked—"Do banks supply
capital to manufacturers and merchants?" They would probably
answer — "Yes; that is one of the objects of their institution."
"Whence, then, do the banks derive the capital which they lend?"
"From their shareholders and depositors." "When you say that
the *currency* is deficient, do you mean that all the gold and convertible bank-notes in the United Kingdom, are not sufficient to
enable merchants to buy goods and pay debts in any part of the
world, provided they possess a legitimate command over these by
having deposits or balances at their credit with their bankers?" We
should like to hear their answer to this question. It could not,
consistently with reason, be in the negative. We should follow it
up by asking — "Or, do you mean that persons who are carrying
on trade greatly beyond the limits of their own resources, and have
no balance of their own with their bankers, find it difficult, especially
when their solvency comes to be doubted, to obtain gold and bank-
notes, on easy terms, to serve them as *capital* in sustaining their
overgrown transactions?" The answer to this question would, we
think, bring out the fact that *currency* has never been wanting to
those who held balances with their bankers; and that it has been
gold and bank-notes to *officiate as capital* that embarrassed traders
have really been demanding.

We should then proceed — "When the banks have advanced in
loans and discounts to merchants, all their subscribed capital, and as
large a portion of their deposits as they should, in prudence, part
with — if these do not suffice to supply the wants of men who are
trading on borrowed capital — is it the duty of Government to come
to the aid of such borrowers' and permit the banks to issue notes for
their accommodation, without reference to their ability to convert
them into specie on demand?" The answer to this question would,
in our opinion, show that the opponents of the Bank Restriction
Act, under the equivoke that the *currency* is deficient, really demand
an unlimited supply of inconvertible bank-notes, which may serve
them as *capital* in maintaining their speculations.

REMARKS UPON THE BANK-NOTE QUESTION IN SCOTLAND.

A PROPOSAL has been made in Parliament to render bank of England notes a
legal tender in Scotland, and one reason assigned for the measure is that when
a commercial convulsion arises, and a severe pressure on the Bank of England
for discounts takes place, the Scotch banks carry off from the Bank one or two
millions of sovereigns, and to that extent diminish the reserve fund of the Bank,
or, in other words, curtail its ability to lend the withdrawn money to its English
customers. Mr. Gladstone calls this a contrivance "to enable people in that
country (Scotland) to go on with a system of investing their capital in securities instead of employing gold, which would not be so profitable to them," and
he "hopes the intellect of England is not so entirely in the background but that
they understand at whose expense this has been done." The newspaper report
bears that this brilliant sally of wisdom and wit elicited "Hear, and a laugh;"
and well it might do so. If the Scotch intellect may venture to measure itself
with the English, we should ask Mr. Gladstone how it came to be in the power
of the Scotch banks to carry off this large amount of specie from the Bank of
England? Does he believe, what his words imply, that the Scotch banks went,
in formâ pauperum, to the Bank of England, and said, "For Heaven's sake *lend*
us two millions of sovereigns, otherwise we must stop payment." No such thing
as this occurred. The Scotch banks held Government securities which, at an
hour's notice, they sold and converted into Bank of England notes, just as John

Jenkins & Co., or any other private holder of Consols and Exchequer Bills might have done, and they sent these notes to the Bank and obtained the gold for them, which the Bank was bound by law to pay on demand. The southern intellect must be sharp indeed if it sees that this transaction was accomplished at the "expense" of England. The fact is, the position of the Scotch banks and of the Bank of England was, in the matter in question, precisely similar;—both were required by their notes-holders to pay their notes in gold; and the one was as much discharging a legal claim from which he had no right to be freed, as were the others. This brings us to the question, What would be the effect of making the Bank of England note a legal tender in Scotland? To answer this question, we must view it in connection with several different sets of collateral circumstances.

The Act of 1844 allowed the English provincial banks, to continue their previous average issues of notes without any security except that afforded by their capital and the unlimited liability of the partners, but beyond that amount it required them to issue only gold or Bank of England notes.

By the Act of 1845 the circulation of every Scotch Bank was limited to its average amount as it stood at that date; and the banks were prohibited from increasing their circulation except on the condition of holding gold for every note issued beyond their average. Let us inquire how these enactments operated.

The Bank of England was bound to pay gold to the bearer on demand for every note it issued. When therefore the English provincial banks put their notes into circulation, they did not impose any new obligation on the Bank of England. They did not force it to hold specie for their accommodation when they wanted it to meet a run. The Bank was bound by law to pay specie on demand for its notes, whoever the holders of them might be.

Let us turn to Scotland. The Scotch banks were required by law to hold sovereigns for every note issued by them above their average circulation. When a run was made on them for gold, they were able to redeem all their surplus notes by means of the gold already in their coffers. When the pressure brought the notes of their average circulation to the counter for gold, how did they meet that demand? They sold Government securities in London for Bank of England notes, and on presenting these at the Bank obtained specie for them. Was any new obligation laid on the Bank of England by this transaction? Did this imply that the Bank had been acting as specie-holder for the Scotch banks, " to enable them to invest their capital in securities instead of employing gold?" And was the gold held by the Bank *at the expense of England,* until the Scotch banks chose to apply for it? It requires not an English intellect only, but a Gladstonian intellect, to be able to answer these questions in the affirmative. It is a sheer delusion to represent the demand of two millions of specie by the Scotch banks in return for Bank of England notes, as an unjust inroad on the Bank's reserve fund; and this will become still more apparent when we consider some of the consequences which would follow from making the Bank of England note a legal tender in Scotland.

First.—Let us suppose that the average issues of the Scotch banks are to be maintained on their present footing, but that for all their surplus issues, now covered by gold, they must in future hold Bank of England notes, and that they may discharge their own debts with these notes as if they were specie. This would be an advantage to the Scotch banks; for with the same funds with which they now buy sovereigns, they could procure Bank of England notes; and these notes could be sent to and from London at less cost of carriage and danger of loss than gold. On the 15th of May and the 11th of November the two rent and interest terms in Scotland, there is always a large temporary increase of issues of Scotch bank-notes, to cover which gold must be brought from London at a considerable expense. In a few weeks, the surplus notes are returned to the banks, the gold is no longer needed, and it is sent back to London. The proposed measure would save much of this expense. Moreover, on the occurrence of an unexpected pressure for money, such as recently occurred, Bank of England notes could be more promptly sent to Scotland by post, than gold by railway.

But what effect would this arrangement have on the Bank of England's ability to supply its English customers with discounts? None whatever. If the Scotch banks by withdrawing sovereigns diminish the reserve fund of the Bank of England, applicable to discounts, it is obvious that, by procuring and holding its *notes,* they would diminish that fund to precisely the same extent; *for the Bank must hold sovereigns in reserve to meet these notes when presented.* The only effects, therefore, would be to keep exactly the same quantity of gold locked up in the Bank's vaults which is now stored in the strong boxes of the Scotch banks, and to lay the expense of the tear and wear of the circulating notes on the Bank of England, which is now sustained by the banks of issue in Scotland !

But, *Secondly*, another supposition may be entertained—viz., that the Bank of England shall be allowed to increase its issue by furnishing notes to the Scotch banks irrespective of holding gold for them. This would be a repeal of the Act of 1844, and would put an end so far to the convertibility of the bank-note into specie on demand. In this case, we should, in our opinion, in times of panic, verge towards the condition in which the people of the United States now are—namely, the holders of these unrepresented Bank of England notes might be met by bank suspension when they required payment of them in specie; our inconvertible currency would then fall below the standard of a gold currency; all exchanges, foreign and domestic, would be deranged; and floods of bankruptcy would overflow the land.

Thirdly,—If it is proposed to allow the Bank of England to issue more notes on Government securities, we ask, Why not allow the Scotch banks to do the same thing? For example, if the £500,000 of circulation extinguished in Scotland by the failure of the Western Bank is to be supplied by Bank of England notes, represented not by gold, but by Government securities, why not allow the Scotch banks to pledge the same securities and supply the void with their own notes? We can see no reason why Government securities, which are regarded as sufficient to cover Bank of England issues, should not be capable of rendering Scotch notes to the same amount equally secure to the public.

Fourthly,—If it is proposed to abolish the circulation of Scotch notes alto-gether, and to replace them by Bank of England notes, these notes must either be covered by gold, retained permanently in the Bank's vaults, or they must be issued on Government securities. In the first case, the Bank of England would be the sufferer, because it would be forced to retain gold equal to the whole average circulation of the Scotch banks, which is at present unrepresented by gold, and which is supported by the security afforded by the capital and universal liability of the shareholders of these banks. If the Bank of England is to be authorised, on depositing Government securities to supply notes for Scotland, why not allow the Scotch banks to continue to issue their own notes on the same securities? If the latter alternative should be adopted, the same rule must be applied to the provincial banks of England, and to all the banks in Ireland; and then we should have the entire circulation of the Three King-doms based on Government securities, with the exception of that part of the Bank of England which might exceed its limit of £14,500,000 now resting on securities. This would be the counterpart of the American system, which has so egregiously failed, and it would render convertibility into specie *impossible* in times of panic.

Or, *Fifthly*, without making the Bank of England note a *legal tender* in Scot-land, Parliament might allow the Scotch banks to cover their extra issues, either by holding Bank of England notes, or gold, in their own option. As long as the convertibility of the Bank of England note was regarded as certain, these notes would be equal to gold in Scotland, and the expense of the transfer of gold would be saved. This rule would impose no new burden on the Bank of England; for the only effect of it would be to allow the Bank to retain in its own vaults the gold represented by the notes sent to Scotland, instead of retaining the notes and sending the gold itself to this country. In case the Scotch people should be disposed to decline to accept Bank of England notes in payment of the obligations of their Scotch banks, they would have the right to do so, and in that case the trouble and expense of bringing gold to Scotland in exchange for these notes would fall on the Scotch banks and not on the public; but this would very rarely happen.

Or, *Finally*, might not the Scotch banks be allowed to employ the Bank of England to act as custodiers of gold purchased by them, and actually deposited in the Bank's vaults, until needed in Scotland! The certificate of the Bank that they held such gold might be received as equivalent to a certificate of its existence in the coffers of the Scotch banks; and by this means the risk and expense of the transfer of specie backwards and forwards to and from London might be saved.

In a subsequent article we shall consider the rate of interest on money depo-sited with banks at call; and try if any sound principle can be reached that should govern its amount.

APPENDIX.

No. I.

TO THE EDITOR OF THE "SCOTSMAN."

198, *Strand, London, December* 12, 1855.

Sir,—Allow me to thank you most cordially for the articles which have already appeared in the *Scotsman* on the Currency Question, and to pray for a continuation of your simple and lucid explanations of other branches in the theory of money and credit. I think, for the clear understanding of this and most other social questions, it would greatly assist if we had a little more reflection combined with the study of past experience and ideas.

I believe you do not consider our present system of currency and banking perfect and past improvement. If it can be shown that any monopoly or influence exists, by which the circulation and value of money is affected otherwise than by the ordinary rule of full and fair competition, and this power is derived from any relations with the Government, you will admit the sooner this connection is dissolved, the better it will be for the community at large. If I may presume to give an opinion, I should say, what we do want is this— in place of the present system of centralisation, we want full and free competition all over the kingdom amongst bankers and money-lenders. With perfect freedom of action, all evils will finally correct and adjust themselves. Who can be so able to regulate the extent of liability or credit between lenders and borrowers, as the persons directly interested? Once allow a third power to interfere, and the prudence and responsibility which should and would exist without this interference, is to a considerable extent paralysed, and becomes day by day more and more feeble. Each individual is or ought to be the best judge as to who he should trust; and as society is made up of individuals, it follows that society or the public is best able to settle all questions of confidence as regards exchange or credit. If I prefer the security of a single person or private bank to that of a joint-stock association, where the directors, with the whole mass of shareholders, are liable for the repayment of my deposits, that must be my own affair, and I alone must be responsible for the result. On the other hand, if I am a borrower, no third power should step in between me and the lender, to limit the amount of credit between us; the lender or bank should be the best judge as to my ability to repay the loan, and would in its turn be responsible for its own act. By an arrangement of this kind, we should have the greatest amount of credit with the greatest amount of security—in other words, free trade in banking.

Now, what I have already stated, and the opinions I have expressed, are based on this one solid condition—the medium of exchange, whatever it may be, by which man lends or borrows, buys or sells, shall have within itself, or represent, some absolute value; and this value shall be of such a character as to be of the most convenient and, consequently, exchangeable kind—such, in fact, as we find in gold!—and into which the medium of exchange shall at all times be convertible; for this power of convertibility is the grand test of value; and unless it will at all times bear this test, its value cannot be maintained. The opinions on the present system of currency, as established by the Act of 1844, may be divided between two classes—one class desiring simply to destroy all existing monopolies, but to retain always the principle of convertibility; the other a class of dreamers and schemers, who never find money or credit abundant or cheap enough to support their gigantic enterprises and schemes. It is to this latter class that the argument of this letter is more particularly addressed. What could be more agreeable to the man of pleasure or the profligate, than some system by which his acceptances could be renewed for all time and without limit—he never having to repay loans of absolute value, excepting with shadows, shams, or wind-bills?

The past history and experience of our inconvertible currency should convince the "doctors" of the danger and evils of such a system; evils not felt at the time, but fostered by a spurious prosperity as false as that experienced by the young extravagant when he has just received an advance from his bill-discounting tailor on his own acceptance, repayment to be enforced some day under great sacrifice and difficulty, or ending in great moral shame, loss of character, and bankruptcy. How can an inconvertible currency command the same value as a metallic currency? The very large amount of money circulating in the shape of wages must, more or less, be paid in metal. Then how can the two work together, unless the paper and metal command equal confidence? Why! Gold and silver will not work together, unless they both have the same market value when they are both by law made legal tender for large amounts. Cheap gold must buy up dear silver, and ultimately displace it, until the silver becomes so reduced in quantity as no longer to compete with gold. Only a few years since, a gold coin was a *rara avis* in France. But what is now the fact? A cab and a sack are no longer necessary to convey the huge bulk of silver in pieces of five francs. Payments are now made in gold, or convertible notes, which may be deposited in the corner of a pocket. The gold discoveries of California and Australia have so far cheapened gold in comparison with silver, as to displace the old silver coinage as a legal tender for large sums. What must then be expected from an inconvertible paper if gold has this absorbing influence over its sister coin, silver? Surely the butcher or the baker will pay more deference to the solid metal, than to the flimsy inconvertible paper.

A sound system of credit must be based on convertibility ; or, what is the same thing, the positive certainty of repayment in acceptable value on demand, and the extent of credit, must bear such a proportion to the amount of existing capital, as to make convertibility a matter of certainty. At the first glance it does appear hard, that such securities as houses and land cannot at all times, and under all circumstances, command credit; but these securities are comparatively valueless as compared with gold or food during a famine. The real signification of credit should be clearly understood—it really means a loan of food, or that which at all times and everywhere, even in foreign countries, is exchangeable for food; and for this purpose we find nothing equal to gold or convertible paper, which may be in truth esteemed as so much condensed food. This credit or loan creates employment for a certain amount of industry. It enables the labourer, by wages, to supply himself with what is necessary for his existence, until his labour is completed, and the results made marketable in exchange for food, gold, or other commodities. It is quite conclusive from this, that the amount of labour engaged in the production of some future results must always be affected by, or bear some proportion to, the quantity of food or gold, that may be in excess over the average requirements of society; in other words, credit must always, to be sound, bear some healthy proportion to capital. Credit based on anything that is not equivalent to, or that at some fixed period will be equivalent to capital, is simply an act of folly, in making the proportions between credit and capital excessive on the side of credit—and, like all errors and crimes, must bear the penalty some day of panic and ruin; in other terms, the quantity of food or gold in stock is not sufficient to support such a large fabric of credit; the food becomes reduced to such an extent as to produce alarm and fear that the results of the labour created by such extensive credit will not be marketable before the stock is consumed; or it may be that, circumstances disturbing the demand, a market can only be made by great sacrifice in value. Hence the demand for time, or an extension of credit, by merchants and manufacturers, who, deceived in their calculations, become overstocked with goods, and can only procure capital at a ruinous price, or by equally ruinous forced sales of their manufactures. Any attempt to keep capital below its natural value by fictitious advances on securities that are themselves not convertible at short dates, is only adding fuel to the fire, by making the amount of credit, as compared with capital, still greater. Much might be said on the causes of panics, and the influence panics exercise on the supply and circulation of capital. Probably there is much attributed to what is called hoarding, as arising from panic, that really should be attributed to legitimate speculation. Gold, like all other commodities, will always fluctuate in supply and demand; and any events, political, social, or physical, occurring, that are likely to increase the value of the precious metals, will invariably give rise to sudden demands by speculators, and for no other purpose than selling again at a profit. Precisely the same operation takes place in respect to corn, etc., etc.; and this is the only true means for preventing the article escaping out of our possession below its value. It is a safe and natural conservative principle, and of great consequence, if not interfered with by influences or powers possessed by corporations protected against free competition by unwise laws.

If what has been stated in this long and, I fear, too obscure argument, is based on sound principles, it follows, that it is not so much an addition to the paper circulation without convertibility that we require, as a full and searching investigation into the relations existing between the Government and the Bank of England, and the power, monopoly, and influence arising out of such relations. As regards the necessity for an extension of credit by an addition to the issues of bank notes, I am of opinion that any direct interference on the part of the Government can only be mischievous, and that every banking association should be able to profit to the full extent of its credit with its clients, and that it alone should be the best judge as to the extent of its issues, the public being protected by the liability of the association, and being secured against an excessive issue by the great and natural principle of convertibility on demand into gold. I am, etc., W. LITTLE.

No. II.

TO THE EDITOR OF THE " SCOTSMAN."

Strand, London, January 1856.

SIR,—I hope I shall not be intruding idly on your space if you allow me to reply to the comments on my letter on the Currency which appeared in the *Daily Scotsman* of December 21. Your conclusion was strictly correct, when you stated that I believe a legal obligation to pay gold on demand is all that is necessary to ensure convertibility, and to protect the public against excessive issues of bank notes. If it can be satisfactorily demonstrated that excessive issues, on which Sir Robert Peel founded his Act, were not the cause of the disastrous bank failures, and, moreover, that with a power of unlimited issue, no bank can increase its circulation at pleasure, you must agree with me that every banking association may be safely left to its own discretion as regards issues, since no Acts of Parliament or any other power can control the circulation, excepting, always, the power of public necessity. The Act of 1844 was undoubtedly intended, by restricting *excessive issues,* to make convertibility still more secure; but it appears never to have occurred to Sir Robert Peel, or those who assisted in framing this law, to ascertain if, from 1819 to the time of passing the Restriction Act, the issue of notes at any time had been so excessive as to explain the cause of the convulsions of 1825 and 1837. A reference to figures and statistics is important evidence when they accord with assumed principles; but if the principles are true, and the reasoning on them is sound, the facts will generally be in accordance.

That banks have no power to contract or increase the circulation, will be at once seen, when it is considered that the medium of exchange or currency is the property of the public, so long as it remains in their hands; and that, accordingly, as they may require more or less of it, they can diminish or increase it at will, in the first case, by simply returning it to the bank, and in the latter case, by drawing on their balances. It must be borne in mind, the public are not indebted to banks for the paper or gold used as currency. The paper is used simply as a matter of convenience; and, taking the entire amount of paper currency, it bears only a small proportion to the value of the deposits and property of the public, which can at any time be converted into currency, if more is required. Currency is simply the instrument by which internal exchanges are effected, whether they consist in payments for labour, food, or manufactures; and any quantity of this medium, exceeding what is actually required, is immediately returned to the bank or source of issue; and it would be just as reasonable to expect that twelve men, engaged in digging, could employ eighteen spades, or even one more than they want, as to expect an over-issue of bank notes to remain in circulation. No sensible man of business keeps a hundred pounds in his cash-box when fifty pounds is all he requires. But if it is not excessive issue that has occasioned the great commercial troubles, where is the cause to be etc., etc.; and this is the only true means for preventing the article escaping out of our possession below its value. It is a safe and natural conservative principle, and of great consequence, if not interfered with by influences or powers possessed by corporations protected against free competition by unwise laws.

If what has been stated in this long and, I fear, too obscure argument, is based on sound principles, it follows, that it is not so much an addition to the paper circulation without convertibility that we require, as a full and searching investigation into the relations existing between the Government and the Bank of England, and the power, monopoly, and influence arising out of such relations. As regards the necessity for an extension of credit by an addition to the issues of bank notes, I am of opinion that any direct interference on the part of the Government can only be mischievous, and that every banking association should be able to profit to the full extent of its credit with its clients, and that it alone should be the best judge as to the extent of its issues, the public being protected by the liability of the association, and being secured against an excessive issue by the great and natural principle of convertibility on demand into gold. I am, etc., W. LITTLE.

No. II.

TO THE EDITOR OF THE "SCOTSMAN."

Strand, London, January 1856.

SIR,—I hope I shall not be intruding idly on your space if you allow me to reply to the comments on my letter on the Currency which appeared in the *Daily Scotsman* of December 21. Your conclusion was strictly correct, when you stated that I believe a legal obligation to pay gold on demand is all that is necessary to ensure convertibility, and to protect the public against excessive issues of bank notes. If it can be satisfactorily demonstrated that excessive issues, on which Sir Robert Peel founded his Act, were not the cause of the disastrous bank failures, and, moreover, that with a power of unlimited issue, no bank can increase its circulation at pleasure, you must agree with me that every banking association may be safely left to its own discretion as regards issues, since no Acts of Parliament or any other power can control the circulation, excepting, always, the power of public necessity. The Act of 1844 was undoubtedly intended, by restricting *excessive issues*, to make convertibility still more secure; but it appears never to have occurred to Sir Robert Peel, or those who assisted in framing this law, to ascertain if, from 1819 to the time of passing the Restriction Act, the issue of notes at any time had been so excessive as to explain the cause of the convulsions of 1825 and 1837. A reference to figures and statistics is important evidence when they accord with assumed principles; but if the principles are true, and the reasoning on them is sound, the facts will generally be in accordance.

That banks have no power to contract or increase the circulation, will be at once seen, when it is considered that the medium of exchange or currency is the property of the public, so long as it remains in their hands; and that, accordingly, as they may require more or less of it, they can diminish or increase it at will, in the first case, by simply returning it to the bank, and in the latter case, by drawing on their balances. It must be borne in mind, the public are not indebted to banks for the paper or gold used as currency. The paper is used simply as a matter of convenience; and, taking the entire amount of paper currency, it bears only a small proportion to the value of the deposits and property of the public, which can at any time be converted into currency, if more is required. Currency is simply the instrument by which internal exchanges are effected, whether they consist in payments for labour, food, or manufactures; and any quantity of this medium, exceeding what is actually required, is immediately returned to the bank or source of issue; and it would be just as reasonable to expect that twelve men, engaged in digging, could employ eighteen spades, or even one more than they want, as to expect an over-issue of bank notes to remain in circulation. No sensible man of business keeps a hundred pounds in his cash-box when fifty pounds is all he requires. But if it is not excessive the gold diminishes. The loans which previously had gone into circulation in the way of purchases, and from the circulation, were restored again to the Bank as deposit, to be re-issued as new notes, are now used for abstracting the gold for exportation, and become cancelled. It is quite clear the greater portion of the fourteen millions of notes is employed, in the first instance, to inflate credit, and afterwards for the purchase of gold for exportation, or, in the case of panic, to strengthen the reserves of country banks.

The following comparative returns of the circulation and amount of private securities for several periods previous to the convulsions of 1825, 1837, and 1847, will show the circulation remained almost a constant quantity, whilst the variations in the amount of credit as shown by the amount of private securities was excessive:—

				Circulation.	Private Securities.
1821	August	.	.	£20,295,000	£2,722,000
1822	February	.	.	18,665,000	3,494,000
——	August	.	.	17,464,000	3,622,000
1823	February	.	.	18,392,000	4,600,000
——	August	.	.	19,231,000	5,624,000
1824	February	.	.	19,736,000	4,530,000
——	August	.	.	20,132,000	6,255,000
1825	February	.	.	20,753,000	5,503,000
——	August	.	.	19,398,000	7,691,000

The above return shows the variation in the circulation from 1821 to the disastrous year 1825 to have been inconsiderable, and in no degree sufficient to explain the cause of the commercial troubles and numerous bank failures of that period; but on looking at the column of private securities, showing the fluctuation in credit, we find it was three times greater in 1825 that in 1821.

				Circulation.	Private Securities.
1833	February	.	.	£19,370,000	£ 5,450,000
——	August	.	.	19,629,000	5,999,000
1834	February	.	.	19,252,000	8,524,000
——	August	.	.	18,839,000	9,688,000
1835	February	.	.	18,328,000	7,870,000
——	August	.	.	17,892,000	11,068,000
1836	February	.	.	18,102,000	11,225,000
——	August	.	.	18,158,000	13,197,000
1837	February	.	.	18,232,000	15,056,000

Taking the returns of circulation and credit up to another period of disaster, 1837, the above table shows the same cause producing the same effect: the circulation is *constant,* whilst the variation in credit is excessive, being again about three times greater in 1847 than in 1844.

				Circulation.	Private Securities.
1844	February	.	.	£21,148,000	£ 5,837,000
——	August	.	.	21,485,000	7,870,000
1845	February	.	.	21,201,000	11,809,000
——	August	.	.	22,109,000	11,712,000
1846	February	.	.	20,968,000	23,242,000
——	August	.	.	21,390,000	12,755,000
1847	February	.	.	20,151,000	15,819,000
——	August	.	.	18,828,000	16,923,000

The next period of commercial convulsion is 1847, *three years after the famous Act of* 1844, which was to prevent future disaster by restricting the circulation. What does the last table show? The circulation is still constant and independent of legislation! But excessive credit is a third time exhibited as the criminal. The private securities are again the incontestable evidence. Can anything be more conclusive that the question of "issue" requires no legal protection or interference whatever, and may be safely left in the hands of bankers and their clients—the public—since neither laws, banks, nor convulsions have any control over it, the supply always being abundantly sufficient for currency or circulation, and being at all times under the control of the public, is always ready to meet the demand? Can it be now said, that excessive issues or excessive circulation was the cause of the great convulsions? Do not the above tables distinctly show, by the fluctuations in the amount of credit as measured by the amount of private securities on which loans had been advanced, that it is excessive credit alone that is the cause of all commercial disasters? And do not they also show that the Act of 1844 is completely powerless to prevent the recurrence of such troubles? From February, 1844, to August, 1847, the circulation remained constant; whilst in the same time the credit increased from £5,837,000 to £16,923,000!

Having shown, by indisputable proof, that it is hopeless to look for any protection against commercial disaster in the restrictions of the Act 1844, and that the only security against the recurrence of such events must consist in the integrity and judgment of bank directors and managers, backed by a more extended and sounder knowledge on the part of the public, it must be granted that a well-conducted system of joint-stock banking offers all the security that can be reasonably required, and that such an association may be safely left to control its own liabilities. The fact of a number of banks having failed from mismanagement, or from any other cause, is no evidence against the security of a system which, under the worst circumstances, would, with reasonable delay, pay twenty shillings in the pound. Ought any doubt to exist as to the soundness and security of the six bank associations in London, when it is known the deposits alone amount to the immense sum of £30,000,000? Could there be any risk in allowing these banks the liberty of unrestricted issue? You have referred to the American banking as offering unfavourable evidence against a system of "free currency" in this country; but I can never admit, because a system of credit may be attended with certain inconveniences in one country, that the same system must necessarily be attended with the same objections in another country. Credit or confidence is one of the highest evidences of social progress; and as neither one nor the other can be had without great industry and consequent accumulation of property, it follows, confidence is a thing of slow growth, and must exist in various proportions in the several countries in the world. But taking America as an example, matters are not so bad as they seem. No convertible State note circulates in the State in which it is issued, below "par"; and the State notes are invariably taken in the way of business, in New York, without any depreciation. Even at the places of public amusement they are accepted at their full value. It is only when they are taken to the brokers or money-changers, that a certain rate of discount is charged for changing them into gold, or notes that pass current in New York. The State banks having no corresponding agents in New York, in the same way that English provincial banks have correspondents in London, on whom their notes are made payable, a charge must necessarily be made by persons who have no interest in taking them. If our own provincial notes were not payable at some of the London banks, they could only be exchanged at a money-changer's, by paying a certain amount for the accommodation: it is therefore a mistake to suppose that American State notes are depreciated; it is, indeed, quite impossible that any note convertible into gold on demand, can be actually depreciated in value. The faintest suspicion as to its integrity would send it to its source of issue, to be tested by a demand for gold. When credit on banking becomes more developed in America, so that every State bank shall have its correspondent in New York, nothing more will be seen or heard of discounts for changing their notes. Under the present system, and in a country so young, it cannot be avoided.

In my former letter, I intended to make a passing allusion to that "crazy question," the fixed price of gold. How much censure Sir Robert Peel might have saved his Act had he been less simple in his definition of the exchangeable value of bullion into coined gold? Had he only said that an ounce of gold, of a certain degree of purity, shall always be exchangeable into an ounce of coined gold, less the cost of coinage, no such "bugbear" as the fixed price of gold could have entered the heads of the "Inconvertibles." Because he employed the money expression of £3 17s 10d., which is the same thing, hence all the confusion about a fixed price. Suppose an Australian digger was to take hs " nuggets " to the Mint, and was to wait until they were converted into sovereigns of *precisely* the same weight, he paying the charge for coining apart, would this be fixing the price of gold? Is the price of bread fixed because the poor man pays the baker a penny for baking his loaf? Is the price of wheat fixed because the quarter is measured by eight bushels? But gold of superior fineness is worth more than £3 17s. 10d. per ounce. Is this fixed? Does not the value, after all depend on the quality, like any other commodity? An ounce of gold may be expressed in coined gold by quantity—as 19 penny-weights and 11 grains; or coined gold decimally in sovereigns—viz., 3·89 or 3 sovereigns 89 hundredths of a sovereign, the fractional parts being equal in value to 17s. 10d.; or in pounds, shillings, and pence—as £3 17s. 10d.; all these expressions being the same thing—raw gold being exchangeable for coined gold less the cost of coinage.

Respect for your space alone prevents me replying by anticipation to the several *imaginary* objections that have been, and will be made, to this free system, such as—the protection of the poor and the ignorant; the absence of secresy in the case of loans by joint-stock banks; how to get rid of the obligation to the Bank of England, &c. &c. Good security, combined with good character, is no beggar, nor fears the light of day. It is this very secresy in private banking that is the cause of so much mischief. Selfishness, or false sympathy, may induce an individual to incur risks by loans on securities at high rates of interest, that would not be looked at by prudent managers of an association, where immediate personal benefit is in no way concerned. Again, hoarding by the poor and the ignorant ought not to exist; and as to insecurity, I should like to know what coin would measure the premium that would be demanded by an insurance company to guarantee security; besides branch banks, or savings-banks, for the poor and the ignorant would set all this right. For the other questions, with respect to the Bank of England's obligation, and for thorough understanding of this, and other interesting matters, I would refer your readers to a recently published pamphlet, by that most able writer and economist, T. Tooke, Esq.*

The proof that no legal enactments can affect the amount of currency, I hope is made sufficiently explicit. That monopolies or exclusive powers must be mischievous, all will admit. This question remains then —Are Acts of Parliaments necessary to ensure integrity and judgment in the conduct of the business of banking? If they are necessary, then Government had better take under its parental control the entire business of the country. No merchant or shop-keeper's transactions should be exempt.

When I argue against any kind of interference on the part of the Government as regards the liability or management of banks, it must not be supposed that I would have no uniformity or discipline in the system of currency that might be adopted, I can readily imagine a system that should give the public the greatest accommodation. If the Scotch system, for example, were employed, the notes issued in any county in England would be exchangeable without the least trouble or difficulty into the notes issued in any other county, and for all purposes of internal purchases or exchange they would have the convenience of the Bank of England note; but all matters of detail might be safely left to the entire society of bankers; the public being their customers, there would be no fear about consulting the public convenience. " With freedom of action, all evils would finally correct and adjust themselves," and we should have the greatest amount of credit with the greatest possible security and convenience; and I firmly believe that it is only the propping up and " protection " given to private banks by the Act of 1844 that has delayed this state of things to the present time. Without this " protection," the majority of private banks would have either been transformed into joint-stock banks, or they would have ceased to exist altogether.

I am, &c.

W. LITTLE.

---

* On the Bank Charter Act of 1844, by T. Tooke, R.S. Published by Longmans and Co.